Lost at the River

Anne Jordan

Copyright © Anne Jordan 2022

The right of Anne Jordan to be identified as author of this work has been asserted by her in accordance with the Copyright, Designs and Patents Act 1988.

All rights reserved.

The characters and events portrayed in this book are fictitious. Any similarity to real persons, living or dead, is coincidental and not intended by the author.

No part of this publication may be reproduced or transmitted in any form or by any means, electronic or mechanical, including photocopy, recording, or any information storage and retrieval system, without permission in writing from the publisher.

Cover/interior design by Liz Carter

This book is dedicated to Home for Good, a Christian charity with a Biblical mandate to care for vulnerable children. Home for Good is dedicated to finding a home for every child who needs one.

See homeforgood.org.uk

Contents

Chapter One	1
Chapter Two	7
Chapter Three	15
Chapter Four	20
Chapter Five	28
Chapter Six	33
Chapter Seven	45
Chapter Eight	60
Chapter Nine	72
Chapter Ten	82
Chapter Eleven	97
Chapter Twelve	116
Chapter Thirteen	121
Chapter Fourteen	128

Chapter Fifteen	139
Chapter Sixteen	145
Chapter Seventeen	157
Chapter Eighteen	166
Chapter Nineteen	172
Chapter Twenty	187
Some Helpful History	191
About The Author	197

Chapter One

Ten-year-old Noah sat in a railway carriage on his own thinking about aunts.

It was the end of the summer term at his boarding school in Leeds, and he was on the way to stay with his Aunt Margaret, who lived in a small town in the country, for two weeks. He wasn't sure about aunts. In fact, he wasn't sure about anyone whose teeth weren't perfect.

A boy in his class had an aunt who visited him sometimes. She had four missing teeth at the front. Supposing Aunt Margaret had missing teeth? That would be bad. After all, it was 1930, and people did have dentists. His own teeth were perfect, white and even.

He had never met his aunt because she had only been back in England a short time after living abroad. He was a bit nervous about meeting her. His dad, who was a doctor, was sending him to stay with her to get over the measles. "Fresh air is good for you," he had said, "just like cod liver oil is good for you."

He was fine with fresh air, but not with cod liver oil.

Noah was glad to get away from his father. Home was not the same since his mother died. He blamed him for that. Doctors should make people better.

The train had stopped at lots of stations, and now there were only three more stops to go. What could he do in the time before his stop? He liked counting, but was there anything in the carriage to count? He looked around him.

Ah yes. He could count the red swirls on the fabric covering the empty seat opposite him. He didn't have to stare at the chair for long, because now he could picture it in his head. He could do that easily. His mind made pictures of everything. It was just like looking at a photograph.

He counted 23 across and 42 down very quickly as he knew the picture in his head would soon fade.

He multiplied the two numbers together, and two minutes later he had the answer, 966. That was a good number. He liked threes and sixes and nines too. But he liked threes the best. Numbers were friends to him.

A few minutes later the train stopped at his destination. As he got off, he scanned the platform for an aunt with missing teeth.

Not one to be seen.

A large number of people were leaving the train now. He counted six porters and a tall thin station master. His mind did its usual picture thing.

The platform began to empty, and he sat down on a seat and waited, watching the train leave. He watched the station master as he strutted back along the platform and then into his office.

"Noah!"

He turned his head at the sudden voice. A woman wearing a light blue dress was running up the platform and waving at him. Could this be Aunt Margaret? No. This woman was too young and pretty to be anyone's aunt.

"Sorry I'm late! My car wouldn't start."

He stared, still not believing this could be his aunt.

"Noah! It's me, your Aunt Margaret."

He stared harder, because all he could see was a big smile full of the best teeth he had ever seen. All the same shape, lovely and white. "Oh, er…"

He was still at a loss for words.

"Not sure if boys like hugs, so I'll shake your hand," she said.

Despite being tongue tied, Noah knew how to be polite. He offered his right hand to Aunt Margaret. She smiled as she shook it. "Good to meet you, Noah. Right. Let's go."

He followed her out of the station, looking around for a car. But there was only one car parked on the street: a Ford Deluxe. He knew that because he had seen one just like it outside his school. Ford Deluxe cars were for rich people.

To his delight, Aunt Margaret walked towards it and opened the door for him. He felt very important as he climbed in. His aunt closed his door, got in the driver's side, and they were off. "It's about 15 minutes' drive to my house," she said, glancing at him quickly. "Enough time to get to know each other. I warn you – I talk a lot."

Noah nodded, still stuck for words.

"I'll start, then," his aunt said. "I own a radio. I live in my own house by the river. I sometimes wear ladies' trousers and I smoke. But don't worry – I'm engaged to the curate from St Cuthbert's church, so that makes me quite respectable." She grinned sideways at him. "Now it's your turn."

"I like rivers," he said after a few seconds, trying his best to sound normal.

"Good. My house backs onto a river. It's called the river Haw and it runs down the back of the houses in the street. Next to it are the ancient ruins of a Saxon church. And next to that is a row of almshouses."

Noah was only half listening. He was still thinking about the river. "Does it have lots of fish in it?"

She smiled. "I can see what's on your mind. You can explore tomorrow if it's a fine day."

Noah said a polite thank you, and both of them were silent for the rest of the journey. Aunt Margaret drove the car down a steep hill and turned into a narrow street edged by a high cobblestone wall. Behind the wall stood a large old church. It made Noah shiver a little to see it, standing there proudly looking out at the town, a large clock on the tower showing the time. It was as if it knew all about him. He took it to be St Cuthbert's.

Aunt Margaret stopped the car at the first house in the street. "Welcome to Low Haw House," she said, smiling her lovely white smile.

As he looked at the house, Noah smiled too, but only to be polite. He was really thinking about the river.

Now that *was* something special.

Chapter Two

That night in bed, Noah thought back over the day. Things had been better than he thought they might be. The relief that Aunt Margaret's teeth had been white and even, followed by riding in a posh car. Then afterwards, she had allowed him to explore the attic. Attics were a gateway to another world, a better one. Then the nice tea he had eaten, and finally, at bedtime, his joy at no cod liver oil greasing his throat.

But the best was to come. Tomorrow he would see the river.

He woke the next day to bright sunshine lighting up his bedroom. He was glad about that. Aunt Margaret had said he would be able to go to the river if it was fine. He got washed and dressed, and went downstairs for breakfast. He had no trouble remembering where the dining room was as he had counted the steps between it and the front door.

The sight of crisp bacon in one dish, eggs in another, and thick slices of buttered bread, was inviting. A big pot of tea decorated with a picture of George V stood in the middle of the table. He filled his plate and began to eat hungrily.

"Hey, whoa there, how about saying good morning to your Aunt Margaret?"

He paused, his fork in the air, and without looking up said, "Good morning. How are you?" Without waiting for a reply, he carried on with his delicious breakfast.

"Ah," she said, laughing. "I should have known not to interrupt a boy and his breakfast."

When he had finished every last scrap of his meal, he jumped out of his chair, scraping it back as he gulped down his last sip of tea. He started to choke.

"Hey, what's the rush?"

"Sorry." He sat down again, coughing.

"I know, keen to get to the river, yes? Go get your tuck from Mrs Horner in the kitchen. I'm going out. See you at lunch time."

In the kitchen, a lady standing at a table rolling out some dough looked up. Some smudges of flour in her hair and a tiny bit of butter on one cheek made her look just a little bit scatty.

She grinned at him, showing a set of teeth with fillings at both sides. A two toothed empty gap at the front made him think of a very dark train tunnel. Best not to get too close – he might get all swallowed up, he thought, and stood himself very tall, preparing himself to run if he had to.

"Eee, yer look reet scared, love! I'm Mrs Horner an' I don't eat children." She laughed, displaying even more of her crooked teeth. "Your tuck is all ready for you."

Noah didn't move.

"Eee, lad, no need to be shy round me." She held a basket out for him to take. He grabbed it and shoved it under his arm. Not stopping to thank her, he ran out of the kitchen into the garden at the back of the house. As he hurtled down the lawn, he heard Mrs Horner calling out something, but he didn't stop until he reached the bottom of the garden.

He had escaped the black tunnel.

He spotted the steps to the river, steep and rocky as they twisted their way down. On each side were a number of purple bushes with a heavy perfume kind of smell. It made him think of middle-aged ladies who came to sports day at school. They were the worst type of aunts.

Taking a step down, he stopped suddenly. He had seen a bee. He didn't like bees. He had once been stung by one and his thumbs had swelled up.

Were there any other bees around? If so, he would have to walk past them to get to the river. Two of the purple bushes spread out across the path in front of him. He couldn't see any more bees… but just supposing? But then he really wanted to go to the river. But then he didn't want to get stung, either.

What should he do?

He thought for a bit. The only way he could get past was to run.

Looking straight ahead, he made a dash for it. He didn't trip once, and in no time he was safely at the bottom. He shook himself. No bees had landed on him. He opened his hands and looked at his thumbs. They looked the same as before. No swelling. What a relief.

And there in front of him was the path that led by the river. And there was the river, bubbling over and dribbling down some rocks as it made its determined way along. The morning sun glittered on the surface of the water, making it sparkle. His mind took a photo of it.

He turned and looked out along its length, the water curving gently towards the bridge he had seen when they turned into the street where his aunt lived. That's where he would go now, he decided. 12 steps would do to begin with, two lots of six. Then he would sit down next to the bridge to see if he could see the end of the river. If not, he would do six more steps and stop again. But first of all, he would just stand still for a moment and listen to the water. And so he did.

After a while, he decided it was time to do the steps he had planned. He set off, counting two lots of six steps as he walked. The path felt good and solid under his feet. After he got to 12 in four lots of three he stopped for a while, sitting down on the bank to look into the water and then watching a group of minnows darting here and there. Then he got up, walked three more steps, then sat down again to do some more staring.

As he got up again, he tripped on something and fell, landing with his head banging on the arm with the tuck box tucked under it. He sat up slowly, his shoulder and arm hurting a little, but not too much. Reaching both hands out, he felt all around him. The path felt smooth apart from a few loose cobblestones. His foot had caught in one of them, pushing the stones to one side. As he tried to put the stones back, he saw some soil heaped up in a small mound. Odd that it should be like that and not flat like the rest of the path, he thought.

As he kicked at the soil, trying to flatten it, he saw something out of the corner of his eye. It was a small bag, pulled tightly closed with a drawstring. He picked it up and shook it to dislodge the soil covering it, and it made a strange tinkling sound. What could it be? Precious jewels, maybe? His hands shaking, he pulled it open and gazed at the contents.

A large number of coins.

He fished one out and turned it over, held it up close to his eyes, and scrutinised it. The writing on it said, 'one penny'. There was an image of a queen's head on it, and he knew immediately who it was. It was Queen Victoria.

Could it be buried treasure?

He looked around to make sure no one had seen him, then slid the tiny bag into his trouser pocket.

Maybe the coins were worth a lot of money? His heart began to beat fast at the thought of being rich. All the things he could buy!

Just then his tummy made a rumbling sound. The walking and digging had made him hungry. Time for tuck, he decided, wondering what treats there would be. Perhaps some chocolate biscuits? They were his favourite treat, thick chocolate and crunchy too, each one delicious.

In front of him was the bridge. He would rest by the wall and close his eyes just to capture a happy picture of what he had seen, and then he would eat. He shuffled forward, sat with his back against the wall, and closed his eyes.

A few moments later he opened them again. Something was strange. It had been sunny before, but now the sky seemed darker, with a low mist rising from the river. He watched the mist, fascinated by its shapes and swirls, then sat up straighter as the mist began to move towards him, closer and closer, spreading first in front of him then all around him as if it were drawing him in. He could no longer see his feet. He was completely enveloped in mist. All he could hear was the low croak of a solitary frog.

A sudden cry made him jump. It sounded close, but the mist was too thick to make out what it was. It was getting louder…

Chapter Three

Slowly the mist began to clear, and a shape took form that wasn't there a few seconds ago. He stared, confused.

It was a boy, about his own age, sitting with his feet dangling over the river, his head bent forward so Noah couldn't see his face. Noah knew he was the one who was crying, though.

Noah took a few steps towards him and then stopped. The boy must have heard him because he suddenly jumped up and turned to see who it was, wiping his eyes on his sleeve. He was wearing rags and shoes with holes that looked like they belonged to a different age. His face was blotched with small red patches, and a white scar ran down his nose to his top lip. He simply stared at Noah, his eyes red, his face paling with fright.

"It's alright," Noah said, taking another step towards him. "I'm not a ghost."

The boy began to back away, his eyes wide with fear.

Noah raised his hand, slowly. "No, stay, please… I won't hurt you."

The boy stopped and sank to his knees, whimpering. "If yer real, don't take me back…"

"I am real… and back where?" Noah said.

"You're not from up t'hill, then?" the boy asked.

"No. I'm… um… visiting my Aunt Margaret." Noah turned, pointing back at his aunt's house. "She lives over there, the other side of the bridge."

The boy frowned at him. "It's a school."

Noah shook his head. "What? No… that's my Aunt Margaret's house. I was just there. I came here after breakfast to see the river."

The boy looked puzzled. Then he shrugged his shoulders as though it didn't matter. "Then yer not been sent t' fetch me back?"

"Um… no." Noah was feeling very strange. The sudden change in the weather and finding the boy whose clothes looked odd and who was frightened of something up the hill. Noah hadn't seen anything scary up there when he had arrived.

Maybe if he talked some more to the boy, he would understand a bit more. He would ask him some questions; three to begin with. That might help him to find out what was going on. "Do you know who the King of England is?"

The boy simply stared back at him.

Noah took that to mean that the boy didn't know the answer. He would try a different one. "Do you know where Germany is?"

Again, the boy didn't answer. Surely he must know the answer to that one, though – after all, England had been at war with Germany only 16 years ago.

"Don't you learn things at school, then?" Noah said.

At this the boy began to cry again. He got to his feet then started to move away hastily.

Noah leaned forward and caught his arm. "No… come back. I won't hurt you!"

Stopping, the boy turned and very slowly shuffled back towards Noah. "I don't know much," he said, stuttering over his words, "an' school were reet bad. It were bad for all us up't hill."

"Which hill?"

"Don't yer know? The one with t' workhouse at t'top of it where I were."

Noah didn't understand the boy's words. People didn't go to workhouses anymore. He looked at the boy, who didn't look mad – dirty, yes, but not mad. It was then that Noah had the first inkling of what might be going on. He reached into his pocket and took out the bag of coins he had found on the path. He poured some of them into his hand, and then he showed them to the boy.

The boy gazed at the coins with big round eyes. "That's enough money for a big shovel full of bread. Yer rich or summat?"

"Oh, is it? Oh yes… well… I've come from a foreign country, see."

"Was yer in Austytralia? Folk get rich over there."

Noah nodded. After all, it was just a little lie.

"I had a mate called Tommy at t'workhouse," continued the boy. "He were sent to Austytralia. He said he were going to get rich by sellin' sheep. He knew about sheep, did Tommy. He said he would send me money to come to Austytralia. Never did, though." The boy pointed to one of the coins. "The pennies are all I know about. I never had any of t'others." He stopped, swallowing as he wiped a tear dribbling down his chin.

Noah picked up one of the pennies and looked at it closely to try and pick out the date. He gulped as he stared at the numbers:

1867.

"18… 67?" he said.

"That's a new penny," said the boy.

Noah studied the coin even more closely, his stomach feeling odd and tight. "Do you mean it's now, or… I mean… has it only just been made?"

"Yep, this year 1867 and lucky too, little 'uns were given free sweets at sweet shops in January."

Noah heard the boy's words, but his brain was racing away. He now knew what had happened. Somehow, he had travelled back in time. He knew all about time. He liked time theories. He had read books at the school library about them.

But how had he gone back in time? The only clue was the bridge. The stones lower down would have been built first. He had gone back to a time when the bridge had just been built. Maybe he had leant back against the very first brick that had been laid down.

How amazing was that?

Chapter Four

Noah wanted to ask the boy some more questions, but the boy was quiet, gazing at the penny with a look of admiration on his face.

"Would you like it?" Noah asked. "Then you can buy some sweets."

The boy began to put out his hand to take it, then drew it back quickly. "I can't, it might be stealin'… an' I'd get hung for that."

"Hung? But you're—" Noah stopped, biting back on the words 'a boy'. Did they hang boys in Victorian times? He didn't know. So instead, he said quickly, "Oh, that's bad." Then, dropping the penny back in the bag with the other money, he slid it back into his pocket.

Suddenly his tummy rumbled, reminding him he hadn't yet eaten his snacks. "Would you like something to eat?" he asked the boy. "I've got some food in my tuck box."

The boy nodded, scratching his nose and then looking up into the sky. A few drops of rain had begun to fall.

"Let's sit down. It's not wet under that tree over there," said Noah, pointing to a large spreading tree.

They sat down on the damp earth, sheltered by the branches, resting their backs against the tree trunk. Noah took the tuck box out from under his arm and opened it, then shared the snacks out between them.

The boy gobbled his share, almost choking on it in his haste. Noah patted the boy's back and then began to eat again. Neither of them spoke. The only sound was the pitter-patter of raindrops tapping the leaves. Noah counted to three over and over again in his head as the rain drummed more heavily.

When he had finished counting nine lots of three, he put the lid back on the box and slid it back under his arm. He turned to the boy. "What's your name?"

The boy whispered something Noah didn't understand. It sounded something like *match*. "Did you say match, or batch, or something else?"

"No, not match, *Scratch*," said the boy, his voice wobbling and then fading as he added, "They called me Scratch at t'workhouse, 'cause I'm always scratching me face. Ta for not laughing."

Noah could only just make out what he was saying. "I won't laugh. It's not good to laugh at things that are not funny."

"Yep. I hate it."

"I'm called Noah. Noah Eaton. Did you have a name when you were with your mum and dad?"

"Me ma died and me dad went away when I was seven to get rich. He said it were for a few days but he never came back. I ended up looking for food anywhere. That's when…" He stopped, wiping new tears away and sniffing. "… That's when I got put in t'workhouse. But my real name is Percy. Percy Shuttleworth."

"Oh, hello, then, Percy. Thanks. My… my mother died too. My father's a doctor."

"Oh yer 'ave a dad then?"

"Yes, but…" He stopped mid-sentence. It was still hard to talk about his father letting his mother die.

"Yer don't 'ave to tell me if it were bad. Any road, yer ma and mine are in 'eaven." He scratched his nose again.

"I don't believe in heaven."

"But yer must believe in 'eaven," said Percy. "If yer don't, what's left?"

"Is that why you were crying and looking crumpled up?" Noah said.

"Can I trust yer to not tell anyone?" Percy said, scratching his chin. "I'd feel a lot better…"

"Yes, shake hands on it if you want. I shan't tell anyone." Noah offered his hand, and Percy nodded firmly before taking it. "But don't tell me too much. My mind has to make pictures of everything, you see."

"Yep, if yer want." Percy sat still for a few moments, staring up at the waving leaves above. "This morning I ran away from t'workhouse. I knew if I got caught I could be beaten or put in prison… but I had to get away."

"Oh… that's bad," said Noah.

"Yep."

Percy continued with his story, stopping every so often to stare into space and scratch his nose. He told Noah he was often beaten by the workhouse schoolmaster. It was because he was slow in learning to read. One child in his class had been beaten to death for the same reason. "I shook all over when that lad were carried out to t'workhouse mortuary."

Noah shivered.

"It's just that I knew that lad. I played sack races with him. When he died, me face itched an 'ole lot more."

Noah didn't know what to say. There were punishments at his school for all sorts of things, but nothing as bad as this. "Are you alright now?" he asked, after a few moments of silence.

Percy rubbed tears from his eyes. "I will be in a minute. Then I'll tell yer one more thing and then stop… 'cause that's enough."

Noah nodded.

Scratching the top of his forehead, Percy took a deep breath then began again. "Night-time were as bad as daytime. We had something called basket drill. We was made to walk around t'room with baskets on us heads which had our day clothes in them. We'd be beaten if us dropped anything. Beds were hard an' all. Yer didn't get much sleep in a dormitory. There was always them that was coughing and them that was whimpering. It meant yer was tired all day."

"So you ran away," said Noah.

"Yes, but if I tell yer how I did it that would take too long, so I'll tell yer another time."

Noah breathed a sigh of relief. "Thank you." He had heard enough for one day.

"Any road, no one's come for me. Guess they think I'm not worth catching. Reckon no one's bothered about a lad who's always scratchin' his face."

"Oh… that's bad," said Noah again after a few seconds of silence. "Or is it good? I mean… it's good that no one has caught you, right?"

Percy nodded, scratched his nose and looked down at the ground. Noah wondered if he would want to be off, but he made no attempt to move. The rain, which had got even heavier, was now easing, the dark clouds moving away quickly and the sun breaking through. Percy lifted his head and looked up at the sky. "Aye, t'sun 'as come out, an' it's made me feel a bit better. Ma used to say that when t'rain stopped a baby would smile for the first time. An' look… there's a rainbow!" He smiled a little as he pointed upwards. "Look how bonny it is. It's like it's dropping its colours on me."

Noah looked up, shrugging his shoulders. He wasn't really interested in rainbows. A rainbow was just something that happened when there was sun after rain.

But Percy was still gazing at it. "I've seen 'em through t'workhouse windows for so long, but I've forgot what a beauty they are."

"It's just a rainbow," Noah replied.

But Percy took no notice. The rainbow looked so beautiful, all clear and bright with its bands of red, orange, yellow, green, blue, indigo, and violet.

"Eee, it's grand. Look at it now! It's like its pointing somewhere. Look… it's tellin' us summat. It's a sign from God."

"It's just a rainbow," repeated Noah, now feeling bored with it all.

"God put the rainbow in the sky after t'earth were—"

"I don't believe in God," Noah interrupted. "That story about Noah and the flood, it isn't true. It's just a fairy tale for little kids."

"Nay, yer can't say that," said Percy, scratching his top lip. "The Holy Bible is God's words. T'vicar at church says so."

Noah didn't reply. He didn't like vicars. They usually talked too much when they came to take school assembly. Now he was even more bored.

Percy kept on staring at the rainbow. "It's come to me, that rainbow 'as. I know now it's a promise for me. All I 'ave to do is follow the rainbow to where it's pointing and there will be a mum an' dad an' a new home reet there. I knows a promise when I sees it. An' that is a promise. I tell yer."

Chapter Five

"Can you say that last bit again?" Noah asked. He didn't want to be unkind to Percy, after all, despite having had to listen to him ramble on about rainbows. "The pictures have to come every time I hear words so I can understand what they mean."

"Oh… it must be like me having to scratch."

"Yes, I suppose so," answered Noah, although he didn't really think it was the same thing at all.

Percy repeated what he'd said about the rainbow, pausing every now and then to scratch or to see what Noah was thinking. "But the rainbow will be gone soon," he said finally.

"Then you won't know where to go," said Noah.

"I know, but I've seen where it's pointing. If I stay near t'river that's where t'new home will be."

"You might get lost," said Noah, thinking the whole idea a bit farfetched.

"I won't if you come with me."

"What, me? Me! I can't, I…" He could say no more. After all, he had no idea how long he would be able to stay in Percy's time.

"Yer don't care, do yer? Yer like them up t'hill. Yer were just pretending to be nice."

Noah shook his head. "No, that's not true. I… it might take a long time. I might have to…"

"What?" asked Percy.

Go back, Noah was about to say, but stopped himself in time. "Er, well… it's just that I'm not good at finding places. And, um…. how will we know when we are there, anyway?"

"Us will know when we get there as that's where the rainbow will be. We can sleep on t'grass. And begging yer pardon, you've got money in yer pocket to buy food with, haven't you?"

Noah stayed silent for a while, thinking. If he stayed in the 1800s, that could be better than his life at boarding school. Aunt Margaret wouldn't miss him, surely – she didn't know him very well, after all. And it would be a good way of getting away from his father forever.

These were good reasons for going with Percy.

"Alright then," he said finally, "I will."

"Ta," said Percy. "Ta a lot. T'good Lord sent yer, I knew it. Like I said, we can sleep on t'grass. An' we can catch trout in t'morning for breakfast."

"Catch trout? Me?"

"Yer ain't caught trout in t'river, then?"

"No, I don't know how. Can you?"

"Yep. Me dad showed me how. Us would sometimes come down t'river to catch 'em reet early in t'morning. That were before me ma died and me dad went away. We never had much money, so a bit of trout did us well for t'day with some bread. I can show yer how to catch one, if yer want?"

Noah felt doubtful. "Alright… um… yes. But how do you cook it?"

"Canst tha' not make a fire?"

"No," said Noah, a little peeved.

"Nay bother. I can show yer."

"I might do it wrong," said Noah, his stomach churning in an unsettling way. Bad pictures were now coming into his head, pictures of him getting burnt and setting fire to the trees. If that happened and they got caught, he could end up in the workhouse along with Percy.

Bending down, he began to fiddle with one of his shoelaces. "I don't feel right about it now… I mean about saying yes to going with you. I might mess up. I might burn things, get us caught. I don't know things like you do."

Percy grinned. "Oh, nay bother about fire an' all. I know about stayin' low. Any road, if us are seen – if that's what bothering yer – you've good shoes to scarper off in. Reckon yer good at runnin'?"

"Yes, I'm alright at it." Noah was good at running. He often won races at school. Some good pictures of receiving prizes were now pushing away the bad ones he had just seen, and he was starting to feel much better. "Race you to the next bridge," he said, looking up, then, not waiting for an answer, he was up and off running towards the path and then straight along it.

The river flashed past him, fresh air filling his lungs, making him feel excited to be alive. Every time he ran, he was king of the universe. He could do anything, go anywhere – even on an adventure. If he was wrenched back into his time now, he might miss something good.

He now knew what he was going to do.

Percy raced after him but could not catch him up. Noah won easily, arriving at the bridge in good time and slumping down by the wall, getting his breath back as he waited for his new friend to arrive. Percy arrived a couple of minutes later, puffing and panting, and flopped down next to him. They sat together in silence as they caught their breath.

Noah was the first to speak. "I left my tuck box behind. But I'm not going back for it. I've made my mind up."

Percy smiled at him, wide-eyed. "So do yer mean yer coming with me?"

"Absolutely," said Noah. "Let's shake on it."

Chapter Six

They had only been walking for a few minutes when a woman walked past them carrying a blanket under one arm. She stopped, turned around, and walked back to Noah, holding the blanket out. Noah gasped as he saw her face. She looked young, but her hair was completely white, and she smiled at him with beautiful white teeth.

Without thinking, Noah took the blanket. Then he realised what he'd done, and tried to hand it back to her, feeling confused and embarrassed. The woman shook her head and pushed it back at him, then abruptly turned and hurried on her way.

Noah ran after her. "Excuse me! This is yours. It's not mine."

The woman stopped and shook her head. She looked out over the river, her eyes reflecting ripples of light from its sparkling surface, and then she softly whispered some words Noah couldn't catch. He waited, shuffling his feet, not sure what to do.

Then she whispered the words again, and this time Noah heard her. "A true witness delivers souls."

What did she mean? The words made no sense to him.

She smiled again and then scurried away, leaving him standing there with the blanket. He watched her go. *Who was she?*

He stood there in the middle of the path, staring down at the blanket, lost in thought.

Percy caught up to him. "What were all that about?"

Noah shrugged his shoulders. "I don't know. She ran away. She said some words I didn't understand."

Percy held out his hands, rumpling some of the blanket in his hands and then stroking it against his face. "It's not like the sort us 'ad in t'workhouse. Them were all scratchy. An' thin. An' they made me scratch more."

"Oh, that's bad," said Noah. "But this is a good blanket. We can cover ourselves with it at night-time."

"Yep," Percy replied, scratching the back of his right ear. "An' about those words that woman said – do yer think they were good, too?"

"Don't know." Noah gazed along the path where the woman had hurried away, but there was no sign of her. "She said something I didn't understand. *'A true witness delivers souls.'*"

"Oh. Souls are to do with church."

Noah didn't answer. He was thinking how well he had done to remember it all. Anyway, he didn't want to talk about church. His stomach was making hungry noises. Sharing his tuck had meant fewer things for him to eat. And now he had money in his pocket to spend – enough for a feast. He turned back to Percy. "Are you still hungry, like me?"

"Yep. I ran off before breakfast, see. A bit of bread and cheese would be 'eaven."

"Where do I buy that from?"

"You'll 'ave to go up t'hill, so I can't come with yer, 'cause I might be seen." Percy pointed back down the path. "Yer know – the one by where yer first saw me."

"How much money will I need?"

"A loaf of bread costs one or two pennies, I think, from t'bakery. Cheese is from t'dairy shop, a few more pennies or so."

Noah nodded. "I'll put those pennies loose in my pocket to pay for it. You stay by that tree. Put the blanket over you to be safe."

"Aye. I will that."

Noah set off, walking back along the path towards the hill. He remembered passing some shops in the town when he had first arrived, so when he got to the top of the hill he headed in that direction.

When he got there, he stood still and stared. It was the first time he had seen a Victorian market square. His eyes took a photo of some of the things he could see. An old woman in the middle of the square brushing a fly away from her face was walking towards three horses standing together, munching on a clump of straw. A sudden splat of horse poo made him screw up his nose and he turned his head away to look at the other side of the market square.

Three small shops stood together, with more further along the road, each with its own sign telling everyone what it sold. He read the signs out loud, letting his eyes rest on the letters in turn. *Harper's Bakery*, the first sign said. Next to that was a bank, and next to that was a black and white building called *The Toby Inn*. He couldn't see a workhouse. Maybe that was behind the shops in the square. He began to walk in the direction of the bakery.

He didn't go in straight away, but stood outside, looking in the window. Cakes, pies, and loaves of bread of different shapes were arranged neatly on shelves. Which one to choose? There were so many. His eyes settled on one eventually.

A few minutes later he came out of the shop cradling the bread under his jacket. He went down the road to the dairy shop, and bought some cheese which he slipped into his pocket. As he paid, the serving woman looked at him in a funny way. She looked him up and down, a big frown on her face, her forehead all crinkled up. He didn't like that. Did she think he was a thief? He had to get back. He was relieved to get outside, and he set off quickly, running towards the hill and then down it. He mustn't leave Percy for too long in case they were in danger. He only stopped a few times to get his breath. As soon as he got back to the path by the river he slowed down a bit, walking quickly back to where he had left Percy.

He saw a heap of blanket with a pair of ragged shoes poking out the bottom. Dashing up to the heap, he bent down and shook it. "Percy, it's me. I've got us some food."

"That were quick," said Percy, emerging out from under the blanket, his eyes sleepy. "Am I glad to see yer. Oh… what's that doin' there?"

It was then that Noah noticed a metal thing with wheels on the path. He could have sworn that it hadn't been there before.

"Oh," said Percy again, jumping to his feet. "Who put that there?"

Noah stared at the mystery object, trying to understand what it was. Nothing came into his head. "What is it?"

"Don't yer have 'em in Austytralia?" Percy asked.

Noah couldn't answer. It was just too much to tell a lie again.

"Well, any road, it don't matter." Percy gave Noah a strange look. "Come an' look for yersen."

Noah approached the thing and looked inside it, gingerly. It was filled to the top with water. He looked at Percy.

"It's alright, yer knows it, don't yer? It's a water cart. Yer fill the metal bucket thing up an' yer push it along with those two handles."

"Can you drink the water? Is it safe?"

"Course yer can drink it. The water comes from t'well. Yer don't get ill from well water."

Noah bent down to have a closer look at the water cart. He touched the wheels. Then he felt all across the bar which the bucket rested on. Finally, he felt the bucket itself.

"'Ave a go pushing it," said Percy.

"Alright," he said, feeling a bit better about it all. Taking hold of one of the handles, he began to push, making sure not to drop the bread which was still cradled under his other arm. He managed a short distance then stopped. It was too difficult.

It was when he stopped that he noticed a piece of paper on the ground. It must have been wedged under one of the wheels. He picked it up and turned it over. Written in small, neat writing were the words: *A true witness delivers souls.*

The same words the woman with the blanket had said to him.

"Look at this," he said, handing the paper to Percy. "It's those words again… the ones that woman said."

"It's nay use showin' me this," said Percy, shaking his head. "I told yer, I can't read much."

Noah read it out loud.

Percy shrugged. "Don't know what the first bit means, but souls are in folks' bodies. It says so in t'Holy Bible."

At the sound of the word *Bible,* Noah screwed the scrap of paper up and threw it in the river.

"What yer did that for?"

"I told you, didn't I? I don't believe in God. And I don't believe in the Bible."

Percy scratched his forehead furiously then put his hands in his pocket. He wasn't smiling. "Well… s'pose that's left to thee to think what tha' likes. Any road… I think that woman left t'water for us."

Noah didn't answer. He couldn't understand how anyone could leave a water cart next to Percy and not be heard. The only thing he could think of was that Percy had gone to sleep.

"Aye," continued Percy, "an' plenty of it to drink with our grub, too."

"Oh yes, I suppose so… only…" Noah trailed off, staring into space, still trying to understand what the words on the bit of paper meant.

"Now then," said Percy, nudging Noah in the ribs, "there's no good lookin' in t'sky for t'answer. Us need to eat. An' I reckon us should find somewhere off t'path again."

The nudge did the trick, prompting Noah to act. He looked around for a place to sit. A shaft of early afternoon sunlight was now lighting up an area of long grass a short way from the path. He instinctively made his way towards it. Percy followed behind, pushing the cart in front of him.

In the grass they sat down together, and Noah took the bread and cheese out of his jacket. "I'll break the loaf in half. Half for now. Half for later."

"Whoa! Just look at that!" Percy's eyes were wide with delight at the sight of the bread in front of him. "White bread, you've gone an' bought white bread! It's only rich folk who get white bread."

"You've not had white bread? Not once, not ever?"

"Nay, mate, at t'workhouse we had bread made with oatmeal. It were brown. It were always dry an' hard to swallow."

Noah wrinkled his nose. "Sounds disgusting. Did it make you sick?"

"Nay, it's all there is. Same stale bread, every day, same every day 'cept Christmas Day."

"That's bad… anyway, I got this cheese too," replied Noah. "But it's not white. Is that alright?"

Percy took one look at it and began to cry.

Noah stared at him and then down at the cheese. "Is it wrong? Is it bad? I'm sorry if I got the wrong thing."

"Nay," said Percy between sobs. "It's perfect. I think… I'm t'luckiest boy to 'ave met yer."

Noah grinned. It was good to do something right. He tore off a hunk of bread and gave it to Percy, who held it in his hand and looked up at the sky for a few seconds. "I was going to say, us should say grace first," Percy said quietly.

Noah knew what grace was, as he had to say it at school, but it meant nothing to him. However, for Percy's sake, he bent his head and listened as he said a simple thank you for the bread and cheese.

Then they began to eat. Chunks of bread and broken bits of cheese never tasted so wonderful. Washed down by hand-cupped helpings of water, it was a feast fit for a king or queen. Even a few spots of rain didn't stop them from enjoying their simple meal. When they were full, Noah wrapped the rest of the cheese and bread in the blanket and stowed it on the water cart.

"Eee, that were better than t'workhouse." Percy rubbed his stomach, grinning widely. Noah couldn't help but laugh, and Percy joined in. "Eee, a good laugh is worth a bit of pity."

Noah didn't understand what he meant, but didn't like to ask. He picked a few blades of grass and began to fiddle with them, tying them in knots.

"Eee, watching yer doing that 'as made me think about all them knotty bits of turnip in t'workhouse broth, but yer don't want to know about that."

Noah looked up at him. "About the workhouse… you didn't tell me how you ran away? Did you climb over a wall? Did you dig a tunnel?"

"Nah, one day when I was bein'—"

Noah touched his arm suddenly. "Stop. Shh," he whispered. "Don't say any more. There's a funny rustling sort of noise. It's coming from that bush behind us. Listen… it's getting louder…"

Percy didn't stay to listen and abruptly leapt to his feet. Grabbing the water cart, he began to run towards the river path. "Run, Noah," he called out over his shoulder. "Them's coming for us!"

Chapter Seven

Noah immediately began to run after Percy, who was now on the path, the water cart trundling along in front of him. There was definitely something following them. *Boing boing*, it went, then *boing boing* again. What was it? He didn't dare look round to see. What if it wasn't human?

Percy picked up his pace even more, running like a wild thing, the water cart weaving and swaying to one side then another as if it might topple over at any moment. He suddenly darted off to the right into a wooded area. Noah followed but could not catch up.

The sound behind followed too.

Percy turned onto a long narrow path which twisted upwards, lined on each side with a heavy green pointed wizard's hat of trees. Each one was blocking the sun out. Noah followed him, shivering despite being warm from the running. The wood had a sinister feel about it. A heavy weight began to crush his senses. There were no mind pictures to help him now.

He began to lose pace. Any other time he would have kept up with Percy but today he had somehow travelled to a different time, run one race and then gone up and down a hill to buy food. He was getting tired. Percy still raced ahead, weaving in and out between trees, the panic showing in his erratic movements. There was no keeping up with him. Suddenly, he darted to the left into a heavier thicket of trees. Noah could no longer see him.

He was alone.

Something was creeping up behind him. A strong smell wafted around him and up his nose. What was it? He searched his brain. Oh yes… of course!

He now knew what was running after them.

He turned around slowly, carefully, and then relaxed. In front of him, slavering and lopping around, was a big blundering dog with ears of two different colours. It dashed at him and jumped up. *Boing, boing,* went its paws, thudding Noah's chest.

Then it licked his face. "Percy," he shouted. "Come out from behind that tree. Come here and face your enemy."

There was silence.

"It's alright. You're safe. Come and look," he shouted even louder still, his eyes scanning the path for a glimpse of his new friend.

Very slowly, a shaky water cart appeared from behind a tree. It was followed by the arms and body of a quivering Percy. Noah ran over to him, the dog following closely on his heels. "We've been running away from a dog, a great big sloppy dog! Look, it's got funny ears."

Percy looked at the dog but didn't laugh. "Watch it, it might be a spy. There were a dog at t'workhouse, nasty brute it were."

"It doesn't look like a spy to me. It likes you. It's licking your hand."

Percy pulled his hand away quickly. "Aye… but it might've smelt me. Yer know… it might've been given summat of mine at t'workhouse to smell. Then it could've been sent off to find me."

"Oh," said Noah, frowning. "Didn't think of that. But if we start to run again it'll just follow, anyway…"

Percy looked even more worried, lines cutting deep in his forehead. He didn't answer, but just backed further away from the dog, who wasn't at all put off. It ambled over towards Percy, and Percy shrank back against a tree.

"I think," said Noah, looking at the dog which was now fervently licking Percy's hand again, "that we are stuck with it. We'll just have to hide here."

"With t'dog with us, yer mean?"

"Yes. We must find a good place to hide. We must tiptoe there. And hope that the dog wasn't followed." Noah didn't wait for Percy to answer. Turning to the right, he made his way on tiptoe into the thicket of trees that lined the path. He could hear Percy behind him, the wheels of the cart squeaking. The steady *plod plod* of the dog's paws rustled the grass as they continued on. Friend or foe, this animal was not going to be gotten rid of.

After a few minutes more trudging on, Noah came to a stop. "Here, look, this is a good place. We can hide behind this tree. It has a wide trunk." He sank down onto the ground, propping his back against the trunk, and Percy flopped down with him. The dog lay down on the grass next to them.

All was quiet now except the rhythmic pants of the dog, getting steadily slower as it fell into a restless sleep. Every so often it gave a little snore. Noah studied it properly for the first time. Nothing was regular about it. Its long legs seemed too long for its body. Its half white-half black face looked like two halves of two different dogs that someone had sewn together and hadn't made a good job. Even its tongue hung to one side rather than in the middle. It just didn't look fierce enough to be an enemy.

Percy's sudden voice broke the silence. "What yer thinking?"

"I am thinking that this dog is alright. It's asleep. An enemy dog would be barking and sniffing around. It's too sloppy to be a spy."

"Yep, I'm now thinking that now, too," replied Percy.

"But don't wake it up… just to be sure. We might be here for a long time."

"Yep, reckon we will. It would be just my luck, run away from t'workhouse then get nabbed by a dog."

Noah nodded his head in agreement. "But I think it's safe to talk so long as we whisper. You still haven't told me how you got away from the workhouse."

Percy grinned. "Oh, that were lucky. I got behind t'velvet-lined door. It were the room where the staff went but us were never allowed in."

"Then what?" Noah whispered back, his voice catching with excitement. "Did anyone see you?"

"Yep, at first, but then… oh! Did yer hear a noise? There's summat moving—"

Noah clutched his arms to his chest, sat very still, and listened. Yes, he could hear something too. This time it wasn't footsteps he could hear but something different. A rustling sound in the grass. His hands began to shake. His racing heart was making his mouth go dry. The thing was getting nearer and with it came a horrible pooey smell rushing up his nose. It made him feel a bit sick.

Then suddenly he saw what it was, moving in their direction, slithering low in the grass. "It's a sna… Percy, a sna…"

"A snay? What's that?"

Noah's pulse pounded at his throat. "Just there, it's… look… there."

Percy looked in the direction Noah was pointing and laughed. "Aw, I see now. It's a grass snake, that's all. Them don't poison yer but they do pong a bit. I do remember stuff before I were put in t'workhouse. Yer not scared of snakes, are yer?"

Noah didn't reply. He hated snakes. He closed his eyes, but it was too late; his mind had already taken a photo of the thing. It was its darting tongue he could see most of all. He opened his eyes, but the picture of the snake was still in his head.

"Oh, yer are! Yer face has gone all white. Best thing to do is back away from it and… now let me think. Yep, got it… sing."

"*Sing*? Doesn't it like singing then?"

"Nay, not the snake, it don't mind about singin'. It's for you. Yep, reckon it will make yer feel better. Do yer know t'song *Ten Green Bottles*?"

"Yes, of course." Noah shook his head from side to side, trying his best to get rid of the snake picture, but it refused to go.

"An' I reckon it's safe t'go now," said Percy, turning to look at the slumbering dog. "No one's come, so best for us to get going again."

Without saying a word, Noah stood up slowly and began to back away. Percy did the same, pulling the cart with him, and that woke the dog up. Shaking the sleep from its body, it trotted behind them.

"*Ten green bottles sitting on the wall,*" Percy sang in a half-whisper, beckoning Noah to join in. Noah's voice trembled as he sang the familiar words. Percy kept the song going, checking all around to make sure they were heading for the correct path. Then, just as they got down to four green bottles, he stopped singing. "Reet then, I think we're there."

A path lay within two medium sized strides of Noah. One, two, he counted in his head, and he was there. Taking a slow deep breath, he turned around, helping Percy with the cart and then patting the dog. He was starting to feel a bit better. The snake tongue picture in his head had been replaced with one of green bottles. Some of them were lying on top of each other. That made him smile. "Which way do we go now?" he asked.

"Well, um…" began Percy, turning his head left and right, a puzzled expression lining his face.

"You don't know, do you? Admit it! You ran so fast, diving in and out, my mind couldn't make a picture."

Percy's shoulders slumped. "Sorry. It were just like… I couldn't see proper… I was scared. An' so I reckon us don't know where we are now."

"That just sums it up," said Noah, sighing as he gazed up at the thick pointed trees. "We're lost in this dark green tunnel. And it's your fault." His words grew louder as he became more aware of their predicament. "We're lost," he shouted, and a ghostly echo bounced back. "*We're lost.*"

Then there was silence.

Percy scuffed his feet in the mulchy leaves for a few moments, then looked up at Noah. "Well, I reckon I deserve that bit of shoutin'. Pa used t'say a bit of shouting does yer good."

"Sorry. It's just… I depend on my pictures coming, you see."

Percy nodded. "Aye, well, no 'arm done." He stood for a while longer in silent thought, then raised a finger in the air. "Oh! It's just come to me. I've got it. That's it! Snakes like water. They can swim."

"So what?"

"Well, it were over there where we were, so it must've come from t'river. So that's the way we've to go."

Noah sighed. "Walk back over there, you mean?" He pointed back to the west, where they'd just come from.

"Yes, but a bit further along, just in case there are any more of 'em. Don't want to scare yer again."

"You really think that the river is over there?"

Suddenly the dog, which had been standing quietly next to Percy, sprang away from them and started galloping along the path. Percy grabbed Noah's hand. "Quick, follow it! We 'ave to follow it. It knows the word *river*. I knows it does. The dog at t'workhouse knew 'uman words."

Percy sprang after it, the cart rumbling along in front of him, and Noah followed quickly as the dog darted off to the west, leading them along a narrow path the same side as where the snake had appeared. "Told yer it was that way," gasped Percy.

Noah didn't reply. He was keeping his head down as he ran, keeping an eye out for more snakes. The dog ran on, both boys following behind. When they slowed down the dog stopped, waiting for them to catch up. Then it trotted off again. "Eee, it even knows when t'go slow," Percy said. "I take it all back. That there dog is a clever 'un, not soppy at all."

Noah just nodded, not taking his eyes off his feet.

Just as Noah felt he couldn't run another step, the trees cleared a little and he lifted his head, looking around. The dark green was losing some of its gloomy colour and giving way to a softer, friendlier green. After a few more steps through a narrow gap he finally glimpsed the river.

The dog relaxed, trotting with them now, sometimes stopping at an interesting smell then ambling on in its lopsided way. Finally, they reached the river with the path stretching alongside it. They had arrived.

It was Percy who shouted for joy first, resting the water cart by a tree and running headlong towards the river, Noah on his heels, happy he no longer had to search for hidden snakes. They flopped down on the riverbank, then shuffled to the water's edge and took off their shoes, Noah his socks too. Then, sinking their sore aching feet into the cooling water, they laughed out their relief as they stared down into its unseen depths. The dog barked with delight and sprang right into the water, leaping and lolloping and swimming then clambering out and shaking water droplets all over Noah and Percy before it did the same thing all over again. Thankfully there was no one about to see or hear them.

They had found the river. They were no longer lost.

"I'm done in," said Percy much later. "We've come a long away on t'path after starting out again."

Noah nodded. "Me too. We've done well in keeping going. Stopping for that bread and cheese definitely helped."

"Aye, an' our water's lasting well. Shall us sit down on t'grass, 'ave a bit more?"

"Good idea."

They cupped their hands in the water over and over again, drinking enough to quench their thirst, then they stretched out on the slope of the warm grassy bank. It was the perfect place to catch some warmth on their faces from the setting sun.

"Even t'dog is flaggerin'. Look at 'im!"

Noah couldn't help but laugh at the dog dozing next to him on its back, making snuffly little snoring noises.

Percy pulled the blanket from the cart and shook it out. "Well, I reckon us three should stay 'ere an' have some kip. This little hill is as good a place as any."

Noah nodded and then yawned, too tired for any more talking. He stretched himself out next to the dog, his back against it for warmth. Percy curled up on the other side, carefully spreading the blanket over the three of them. "Reckon t'dog is wanting to stay with us," he said sleepily.

"Yes," replied Noah, trying to smother yet another yawn.

"Reckon we should give it a name. What about Lolly? It's always lolling about the place."

"Yes, nice," mumbled Noah, his eyes starting to close. "And tell me… what's 'flaggering' mean?"

There was no reply. A few seconds later he heard a low snort, then some clicking noises, then a gentle snore.

He felt himself drifting off and allowed sleep to swallow him up.

In no time he was back at school, sitting at his desk. The classroom walls were moving. He knew he had to get out, but he was stuck to his chair.

Then a dog bounded up and the walls fell into a heap of rubble, and then he was outside, the wailing wind moaning around him. He tried to move his hands over his ears to block out the noise, but they would not move.

The walk back from swimming lessons had been so cold his hair was stiff with frost. A white figure appeared and began to scratch his frozen head. "Nits," said the figure.

"Sorry, Matron."

"You must have a bath."

A bath appeared from nowhere and then grew bigger. He knew he had to get into it with everyone else. Three inches of ice-cold water. Boys around him were fainting with the shock.

A plate appeared out of the water, held out by an armless hand. On the plate something solid and black squirmed from side to side.

Every Tuesday they had to eat it, school liver; gummy, bitter and served with slimy onions. It began to move towards his mouth, and he tried to close it but couldn't. The horrid stuff exploded into his mouth like rising steam from a fast moving train, filling every space until he choked and choked and screamed and screamed and—

"What were that?" Percy said, waking up suddenly and sitting bolt upright.

"Sorry… it's me," Noah replied shakily.

"Eee. I thought me end 'ad come. Yer scared me back t'workhouse just then, with that screaming, bad dream or summat?"

Noah shook his head over and over again to get rid of the picture he had seen in his nightmare. It made him feel sick. "It was horrible… I was back at school."

"Oh. I reckon us need to sing again."

"What, *Ten Green Bottles*?"

"Yep, but yer can change words, yer know. Yer can sing *ten bowls of gruel hanging on t'wall* or *ten dead chickens hanging on t'wall*."

"How about *ten plates of bread and cheese hanging on the wall*?"

"Alright, but can us start at five? I need some more kip."

"Agreed."

Only the river and the dreaming Lolly heard two boys singing about five plates of bread and cheese about to fall off a wall. It was enough to relax them both, and they soon fell into a deep sleep.

Chapter Eight

Noah woke up first. He had slept well after the fun of singing the green bottles song. Sitting up and looking around, he listened as a bird trilled its joy at the start of a new day. Thin streaks of dawn sunlight were beginning to break up the night sky, demanding the darkness to go.

Percy, who had rolled over in the night, was now curled up with one arm resting on a raised gnarled root of a large tree. Lolly was down by the river, sniffing fresh morning smells. Everything was quiet and peaceful.

Noah was so taken up with it all that he didn't see Percy get up and approach him. "Grand, ain't it? I used to come fishing with Pa before he went away. Trout is best caught in t'early morning."

"Better than school."

"Like us said before, we can have a go at catching a couple for breakfast. Pa told me some of the best hours of t'day to catch trout are before t'sun comes right up."

"Oh?" said Noah, shuffling over slightly to watch a large bird who was perched on a low branch overhanging the river, staring into the water. It was unmoving, like a statue.

"Yer not listening, are yer? Yer watching that heron over there."

Noah nodded. "Is that what it is?"

"Aye. Before t'workhouse got me, I loved nature. Them herons are good at catching fish. All they do is sit an' stare. They just sit. Then when they see summat to catch they move their heads side to side."

"Doesn't it make them feel dizzy?"

"Nay. I 'spect it's so they can see better. They dive in when they see a good fish and then spear it through t'body with their bill."

"That's horrible," Noah said, screwing his face up tightly.

"Reckon it's over quick. S'pect fish feels nowt about it. Any road… time for us breakfasts. I just wondered… how about yerself having a go at catching a trout?"

"I won't have to spear it?"

"Nay, it's more like playing than spearing."

"Alright."

Lolly ambled over and trotted along with them as they made their way to the water's edge. Percy led Noah to the bank. "Right then. Yer looks for trout under overhanging bits of t'riverbank – so get looking."

Noah peered over all the overhangs he saw as he walked slowly along the bank. "What do they look like?"

"Brown trout have yellow underbellies, not pale yellow but bright like t'sun an' brown spots on top. An' no noise… keep quiet as yer move, it's best to tiptoe."

"Sorry," whispered Noah, beginning again and staring closely into the river as he tiptoed along. It was difficult to tiptoe and look at the same time, but he was determined to do it. After all, he had agreed to do everything with Percy on their adventure together.

Then, just as he thought he would never see one, he saw something out of the corner of his eye. A trout! Could it be more than one? "Look Percy – down here," he whispered, lowering himself down onto the grass.

Percy looked over into the water and grinned. "Aye, that's it, an' a pair too, now that don't happen much. Them trout like to swim alone in t'summer."

"What do I do now?" Noah asked.

"Bend over reet down under that bit of bank. Use one hand to get underneath the fish an' work yer fingers from t'tail upwards," Percy whispered.

"What if it moves?"

"Keep quiet, you'll be fine. Now then, just use the tips of yer fingers an' tickle its belly. Keep steady now."

Noah dipped his hand into the river. The water was colder than he expected but he kept as steady as he could and did exactly as he had been told.

"Once yer can reach t'head, grip hard an' lift fish out of t'water. Just watch it if it's a big 'un… it'll start fighting an' then might bite."

Noah nodded, keeping his eyes on the fish and slowly moving his hand towards its head. He gripped the trout as hard as he could then hurled it onto the riverbank where it floundered there in the early morning sun, stunned.

"Ah that's grand, tha's done this before."

Noah grinned, slumping back on the bank and admiring his catch.

"Right. Keep still… I'll get t'other one."

In no time there were two freshly caught trout lying next to one another. "How do we cook them?" asked Noah.

"Yer cook 'em on a stone near t'fire."

"A fire… how do we do that?"

"Don't yer 'ave fires in Austytralia? Oh, course not… it's too hot, ain't it?"

"No, I mean… yes," Noah answered, his face beginning to feel hot. It was getting harder to lie. Percy was now his friend. He should be brave and tell him the truth. But how, he didn't know. Probably best just to say it as it was.

He took a deep breath. "Percy… listen. I have something to say about Australia. I—"

"Tell us later. Food first."

"After breakfast, you mean?"

"Yep. Now yer can help me get some sticks to make t'fire – dry ones, yer know."

"Alright then." He had escaped telling Percy the truth for the moment, but made a silent promise to himself that one day soon he would.

They went to look for dry sticks and soon had a bundle each. They stacked them up together and then Percy said he was going to look for some stones. "Grab two of them sticks an' start rubbin' them together," he shouted back over his shoulder. "Back in a jiffy."

"How long for?"

"Yer keep going till yer arms ache. Sing *Ten Green Bottles*. It takes yer mind off it."

Noah took two of the sticks and began rubbing them together. It wasn't long before his arms began to ache. He began to sing, but it did nothing to help his aching arms. He was relieved when Percy came back with several stones.

Dropping them on the grass, Percy laughed. "Yer look done in."

"It's hard work doing this."

"I can tell tha's not a Yorkshire lad. Give 'em to me."

For a minute, Noah felt cross – after all, he had never made a fire before. Then he began to see the funny side of it. What if Matron could see him now? All those flying bits from the sticks going up his nose and making him sneeze. It would have meant pink medicine at bedtime for days. He grinned to himself as he handed the sticks over to Percy, who knelt on the ground and began to rub furiously. Noah watched in awe. Percy didn't need to sing as within a few minutes a tiny spark flickered into being. Percy laid the sticks on the pile then added more small sticks and some dry grass on top.

They waited. Then they sang one round of *Ten Green Bottles.* Then a small flame appeared, and then grew, gradually flaring into life and licking at the sticks and grass. Percy added more sticks on top and within a few more minutes they had a small fire. Percy placed each of the fish on a decent sized stone as near to the flames as he could.

"How long will they take to cook?" asked Noah.

"It flakes when it's done. T'colour goes pale. If we sing *Ten Green Bottles* then *Ten Dead Chickens* a few times it'll take up t'time, an' then we can try 'em."

"We have some bread left too, and some water."

"Yep. Start singing. We'll 'ave breakfast while t'sun gets up."

Not long after that the fish was ready, and the bread broken up between them. Lolly was busily eating something he had found by the river.

"Now then. All us need to do is say grace, alright?"

"Go on then." Noah listened as Percy said a simple thank you prayer.

For Noah, breakfast in the early morning sun never tasted so good. Could anything be better than this? He licked all the fish bits off his fingers and laughed, because his father would never approve of such a thing. "Licking your fingers puts dirt into your body," he would have said with his lips curled downwards.

"What yer laughin' at?" asked Percy.

"My father." Noah explained why.

"Nowt wrong with a bit of dirt. Eaten enough of it mesen, an' still 'ere."

Noah nodded firmly in agreement.

"Enjoying a bit of breakfast then, lads?" A sudden voice behind them made them jump. They hadn't heard anyone coming. They turned their heads and saw a tall, stooped man with a large head and big hands dressed in old, brown-stained clothes. A smell of farm muck hung around his body. "Mind if I sit down?" he asked.

Not waiting for an answer, he crouched down close to the dying fire and rubbed his hands. "A fine morning, ain't it? You look like two lads who like being outdoors."

Percy edged away slightly.

"So, are yer both from round 'ere, then?"

Neither of them answered.

"Saying nowt, is it? That's not the way to talk to a gentleman. Especially as yer will be getting to know me reet well." He stood up and looked down at them, a cold grin curling his mouth. "Fishing's over now, lads. Both of yer are comin' with me. I need two more to join t'others, an' if yer don't shift I'll just get t'master from t'workhouse. He can get yer a nice 'ome, he can."

Noah couldn't move or speak and his stomach churned. Percy too was motionless. They stared into the face of this stranger, transfixed.

"Get up an' follow me. An' no shoutin' out. Yer next meal will be a reet good treat." He bent and grabbed Noah's ear, then Percy's, and dragged them both to their feet. "An' don't yer dare try an' run. I 'ave my spies lookin' out."

Noah and Percy stood still and silent, not daring to look at each other. Noah's ear was stinging.

"An' the dog stays put. Got that? I've got a real nice dog for yer both to meet. I'll just make sure this one 'ere don't follow us." He went to the water's edge and grabbed and then started to beat Lolly, who backed away, yowling in pain and outrage.

"Leave him alone," cried Percy, running towards the cowering dog and throwing his arms around his neck. Then he whispered something in his ear. "He won't follow now, I know it," he said a few seconds later, looking the man directly in his face.

"A dog whisperer, eh? Well, yer might be useful with horses. Right. Let's get goin'."

Noah and Percy both knew without saying a word to each other they had no choice but to leave Lolly and everything else behind and follow the man. They trudged after him, miserable.

After a few steps, Noah stopped and ran back to give Lolly a last hug. He knew by the heavy sound of the man's footsteps that he was close on his heels, but this time he thankfully left Lolly alone. Noah's heart lurched inside him when he saw the look of bewilderment in Lolly's big brown eyes. He knew then that he would never see him again. He would never forget the dog who had given them so much laughter and faithfulness.

"Get moving," the man said, and he turned back and followed him along the path with Percy. He had a heavy feeling in his chest. Starting off to look for a new home for his new friend had been an adventure. But now it was all going wrong.

And what about himself? Noah Eaton? Was he now lost in a century he didn't belong in? Was he lost at a river which only a day ago had been a good friend to him? And what about Aunt Margaret?

Would he ever get back?

It was soul destroying to be walking back the way they had come the previous day. They followed the man away from the river into the wood where they had seen the snake. The sky was bright, but under the trees it was dark, still and lonely. They trudged on until they came to a narrow country road. There, standing a little way off, was a skinny horse attached to a cart, munching something it had found on the ground, its thin jaw trembling with the effort. The man ignored it and jumped up onto the cart. Noah and Percy stopped and waited a little way off, staring at the weary-looking horse.

The man scowled at them. "Don't just stand there. Shift yer behinds. One this side of me an t'other get in other side."

Percy climbed up on the far side of the cart, leaving Noah to get in next to the man on his side. The man snatched up the reins, then snorted a throaty "gee up" which startled the horse into moving and jerked Noah and Percy backwards. "Nice little journey for yer lads on a summer's day," he chuckled to himself as they trotted along.

Remaining silent, Noah and Percy looked straight ahead.

"What, no thanks for me kindness, then? Nay manners. Yer'll be giving me a bit of respect soon, 'specially at supper time, yer know."

Noah doubted that, and guessed Percy did too.

Chapter Nine

All was quiet now except the rhythmic *clip clop* sound of the horse's feet. Eventually they came to a fork in the road and turned right, where the road widened and then curved over a narrow stone bridge over a stream. At the other side of bridge the man wrenched the reins, dragging the cart to a halt. "Get out," he ordered.

They jumped down to the ground.

"The rest of it is on foot as 'orse can't get there. It'll find its own way 'ome. Reet then – we go down that way." The man pointed to a path alongside the stream.

The sun was high in the sky as the boys trudged on, following the man down the path and then branching away from it. Noah scarcely noticed what was in front of him as he kept his head down, simply following in the man's footsteps. He didn't look at Percy, knowing full well that he was experiencing the same despair. The man neither looked around nor spoke to them. His long strides meant they had to hurry to keep up with him. Soon they were marching through open fields, and a little further on they reached a field with a scattering of buttercups where the man suddenly stopped.

He turned to them and grabbed them both by one ear. "Reet then. If yer ever talk about what yer going to see next I'll dunk yer face in a ditch of water an' keep it there. Got that?"

Noah and Percy both nodded together.

He let go of their ears, making Noah lose his balance and fall over. As he got up, he made to kick the man on his leg, but the man caught his arm and shoved him down on the ground again, growling, "Don't yer ever do that again."

"Sorry," Noah stammered.

Muttering something Noah couldn't hear, the man turned and began to walk off. Noah and Percy had no choice but to follow.

As they trekked through the field of buttercups they eventually saw a thick clump of trees at the far side. They came to a wooden stile in a fence separating the field from the next one. The man jumped over the stile and Noah and Percy clambered after him, Noah's arm hurting from when he'd fallen. The man led them onto a narrow track with wheat growing either side.

After seeing nothing but fields for what seemed like hours, eventually they spotted a grey brick farmhouse in the distance. It had five windows and a smaller buliding attached on one side, with a small garden in front surrounded by a low stone wall. A gap in the wall took the place of a gate.

They made their way towards it, and as they approached the garden the man turned to face them. "Welcome to Hugh Moor Farm. If you don't like it yer off yer 'ead. Yer 'ave some new mates, too. Follow me round t'back."

They made their way around the back of the house and stopped and stared at a group of dirty children and a few women. Noah did a quick count in his head. 23.

The man stood with his arms folded, looking straight at Noah. "Here we are. Meet yer companions." No one in the group moved or smiled. "I'll show yer what 'appens to them who don't do what I says." Grabbing hold of the nearest boy, he whacked him hard round the head. The lad fell over, but no one moved to help him. "Reet then, rest of yer get going. I'm off for me breakfast. Got to feed a rumbling belly." The group quickly scattered in all directions, and the man waved back at the lad on the floor as he strode away. "He'll tell yer what to do."

As soon as he had gone, Percy and Noah ran across to the howling boy and helped him up, propping him against a wall. "What's your name?" Percy asked.

The boy swallowed. "Ha… Harold."

They crouched down with him, waiting until he had calmed down a little. Percy told him their names and the story of how they had been kidnapped.

Harold looked them both up and down. "I would've taken yer both for brothers if it weren't for t'clothes yer wearing. Like them short trousers you've got on."

Noah hadn't thought about the fact he was wearing 1930s clothes.

"I thought t'same when I first saw him. But he's from Austytralia, and that's special," said Percy.

"Oh, that's alright then, it's a new world over there. An' it's upside down," replied Harold. "I know all about that, onions an' all."

Noah couldn't speak. A picture of onions was forming in his head. It was as bad as liver.

"Onions?" said Percy.

"I 'ave a couple of 'em from top field for me supper at night. Them grow right way up."

No one said anything.

"An' now yer both want to know why yer here?" Harold said after a pause.

"Mmm," replied Noah, shaking his head to get rid of the onions.

"It's 'cause he needs two more kids to do t'jobs that Freddie and Lenny did. They were my twin brothers." He gulped and looked down at the ground. "They're dead. An'… an' it's 'cause of him. The gangmaster."

"Dead?" whispered Percy, scratching his left ear.

Noah felt something cold creeping down his back.

"Aye. Some farmers take gangs on to do t'work on t'farm. I know all about it. The gangs are organised by a gangmaster who goes round and asks poor kids and poor women to work for him. He says it's good money… so us have to agree."

"The man who brought us here… is he a gangmaster?" asked Noah, still trying to blink away the onions.

"Yep. What happens is he goes to a farmer and says he has this gang who will work on t'farm an' he asks t'farmer how much money he'll get paid for getting t'gang together."

"So it's like selling people?"

"Aye. Farmer says what he will pay, an' they agree on t'price. An' then us have to do what t'gangmaster says an' he pays as little as possible an' we have to work nigh to fourteen hours a day."

"And do you sleep here?"

"Nay, yer sleep at 'ome if yer 'ave one. Ma said I had to earn money to buy us food. Ma says she has too many hungry bellies to feed. That's what she says when she's sober. Most of t'pennies I gave her went on drink so now I save 'em up an' pass 'em to one of t'women yer saw. She buys bread for me brothers and sisters."

"Oh, so you don't go home, then?" Noah asked.

"Nah, home's no good. Freddy and Lenny died 'cause they got sick at home and Ma said they had to get back t'farm... an' they did..." Harold stopped, sniffing. "... An' they died in t'fields picking stones."

A solitary cow in a nearby field began to moo, its long mournful notes reflecting the sadness they were feeling. Another cow joined the lament.

Harold was silent for a few moments, staring up at the sky. "It were a hot day," he continued. "What with not much food and no water an' being sick they fell down dead straight on t'grass... an' when I turns 'em over... Lenny had bird poo on his face."

"Oh, that's horrible. You... you don't have to do any more talking if you don't want to," Noah said forcefully. Somehow, his mind was now making pictures of onions smeared with bird poo.

"Nay I will, 'cause you'll get to know any road. It's right bad for us. When t'gang are working a long way away, the children leave at five in t'morning and it can be eight at night for them get 'ome. An' then they have to do t'same next day. Aye... wait." He sat up straighter, turned his head on one side. "Hush up a minute... I thought I heard a noise. He might be coming back."

Noah listened, but there was no sound except for the occasional sad moo from the cow.

"Jobs depend on time of year," continued Harold. "Some of us have had to be live scarecrows an' to run up and down t'fields all day chasing birds away so as they don't eat t'seed when it's planted—" Harold stopped short again. "Oh… hush… I definitely heard a noise this time. We'd better get going."

"Where to?" Noah asked, looking around.

"Follow me." Jumping up, Harold took off towards the back of the farmhouse. They followed behind him as he led them to a field a little way from the farm. He sank down on the grass, and Percy and Noah flopped down next to him, puffing and panting.

"I'll finish telling yer what I was going to say about us jobs, but then we have to get working. You two keep a look out."

Noah was feeling wretched. All he could do was listen and hope no more pictures would come. He was also surprised that Harold could do so much talking after a hard hit on the head.

"Reet now… where were I?" said Harold, after getting his breath back. "Oh, yes. So, some of us have to pick weeds by hand. An' there's helping with t'hay an' muck spreading and planting taters.

Yer needs to be able to run fast and bend down to t'ground. The gangmaster will beat yer if you don't work fast enough."

Noah took the chance during a pause to try and catch Percy's eye, wondering why he hadn't said anything for a while. Never had he seen anyone look so helpless, and he suddenly felt very angry. "He'll not keep us here. We'll run away, both of us."

"Didn't he tell yer about the dog?" Harold said, giving Noah a long stare.

"Yes," Noah said, sighing.

"They say it will tear yer to pieces if yer get anywhere near it. He keeps it in t'cowshed."

Noah felt himself starting to shake.

"Aye, it's a terror to see, they say." Harold thumped the ground with his fist. "Nay. Yer stuck here now, picking stones with me, an' we'd better get on with it."

"You mean like Freddie and Lenny?"

"Yep, just like they did. Yer pick stones in fields that have no crops growing in 'em. T'farmer wants no stones to get in t'way of his plough. A stone can do a mischief in t'works. Fields have to all be clear so he can sow seeds for next year's crop."

So that was it, thought Noah. Picking stones all day, every single working day. This was their life now. Looking around at the field he was in, it felt like an impossible task.

"That's what I did when I first came an' I were told what to do. I looked around and I says to mesen, that's me life now, onions an' all. That's it… there's nowt else."

Noah edged away, feeling thoroughly sick. He began to heave, and then groaned as all his breakfast bread and fish splattered out onto the grass.

Chapter Ten

"It's worse than t'workhouse," Percy gasped. "At least yer got to sit down sometimes, like at school an' mealtimes."

They were slumped by a hedge, eating their meagre lunch of dry bread and cheese. Noah nodded, too tired to speak, having filled a wooden wheelbarrow with dry stones. His back ached so much from bending down that he had started to pick them lying flat on his stomach. His fingers were now aching so much he was finding it hard to keep hold of the food. His mouth was so dry it was hard to swallow. Oh, for a long drink of water. The tiny bit he had been given wasn't nearly enough to quench his thirst.

And they were only halfway through the day.

"Right, us have to get back to work," said Harold a few minutes later, draining the last bit of water from his can. "Or he'll see us idling an' he'll be down here with his belt wrapping round us backsides."

Slowly and painfully, Noah and Percy stood up and followed Harold back to where they had been working. Noah eased himself down on the grass and began the tedious work of picking stones once more.

It only seemed a few minutes later that Noah felt a sudden shaking sensation on his shoulder. His eyes snapped open. *Oh no*, he thought, *I must have been asleep*. He sat up straight away. A young girl with red sore eyes was standing there, just looking down at him. Noah could tell that she had been crying. She was small with light gold-brown hair and large brown eyes. Her dark green dress made Noah think of his mother, whose favourite colour had been green. He swallowed a lump in his throat. "Hello," he said with a catch in his voice. "Are you lost?"

"Yes… that man up there stole me," she sobbed. "He brought me here. Then he left me. He said you would tell me what to do."

It was a sad, frightened voice. Noah's heart lurched within him. Had this poor little thing been taken away from her family to work in the fields? The gangmaster must have just left her here whilst he had been dozing. It was surprising that he hadn't given Noah a belt round his backside for falling asleep. Maybe he had thought she would try to run away?

The little girl's tears were flowing faster now.

"Don't cry, I will be your friend," said Noah, pulling up a handful of grass and handing it to her. "Sorry it's not a handkerchief, but it's all I've got."

The little girl took hold of the grass and began to wipe her eyes.

"What's your name?" Noah asked after giving her plenty of time to dry her tears.

"Molly. I'm seven."

"I'm Noah," he said, trying to make his voice sound cheerful.

"Are they your brothers over there?"

"No, they're my friends, Percy and Harold. We work here, picking stones."

"Is that what I will have to do?"

Noah didn't answer. How could he tell her that she would have to pick stones all day with little food and water? How could anyone expect a little girl to do that? And he definitely didn't want to mention the brute savage of a dog that would chase her if she tried to run away.

A lashing of blood red anger suddenly raced through his brain. "No, this is all wrong. You're a girl. I won't let you do it… Oh! I have an idea. Lie down in the grass by that hedge over there. On your tummy."

"Like this?" Molly threw herself down on the ground.

"Yes, and wriggle along the ground a bit. Like you're pretending to be a snake. Keep as low as you can. The ground dips a bit so the gang… the man might not see you." Noah looked around and lowered his voice. "Now go, before he sees us talking too much."

Molly tiptoed over to the hedge, bending low, and found a spot to lie down on her stomach. All Noah could see of her now was her dark green dress blending with tufts of lighter green grass. There was a good chance she wouldn't be seen.

"Who was that?" Harold's sudden voice behind him made him jump. "An' lie down, yer can be seen for miles."

Lowering himself back down onto the grass, Noah began to tell Harold all about Molly. Harold listened without interrupting, a grave expression stamped on his face. "I know it's bad, but she's not t'first," he said when Noah had told his tale.

"You mean the gangmaster employs tiny little girls like that? I mean she says she's seven, but only looks about five."

"Yep. They're nearer t'ground than us bigger ones. Little fingers can see tiny stones that us miss."

"But… working all day like that, it's bad enough for us lads."

"Aye. An' if yer can think of a way to get us out of here then I'm all ears but it won't be easy. It could be blinkin' hard, onions an' all."

"Yes, and she's only got little legs for running."

Harold nodded. "Too true, but better get back to them stones afore we get nabbed idling. I'll wriggle my way up t'Percy on t'way back an' tell him about Molly."

He was gone before Noah had time to answer.

In the early evening, Noah slumped down alongside Percy and Harold, their backs propped up against Molly's bit of hedge. They had found her fast asleep after they'd worked in the field all afternoon. They didn't wake her. They had some food and water for her for when she woke up, stowed in a shady spot nearby.

"Oh, jigger it, I'm so fried up," said Noah after a few moments of getting his breath back. Leaning further back into the hedge, he breathed out slowly.

"What?" asked Harold. "What's fried up?"

Noah felt his face suddenly go hot. A boy at his school always used that phrase to mean he was tired out, but it might not be a saying people in Victorian times knew.

"It's probably Austytralian!" said Percy.

Noah's stomach sunk. It was no good. He couldn't pretend any more.

Taking a long breath, he began to tell them about himself. He told them what 'fried up' meant. He told it all, only stopping at the point in time the gangmaster had kidnapped them.

"Now you know it all, you can stay away from me if you want. I expect you think I'm mad, anyway."

Neither Percy nor Harold spoke.

He sighed. "That bad, then."

"No," said Percy eventually. "I don't care if you're off yer chump or summat, though I don't think yer are 'cause yer talk clever an' yer good. I can tell that as yer work yer guts out picking stones. An' yer chose to help me at t'river. Us Yorkshire folk know goodness when us see it."

"Same here," Harold said.

Noah felt a huge lump in his throat. He had never known real friendship before. All he could do was stammer his thanks.

"I'm fried up, too," said Percy a few seconds later, sinking further back into the hedge.

"An' me," said Harold.

Just then Molly made a murmuring sound and opened her eyes. She blinked and looked around with a startled look on her face. Then she settled her gaze on Noah.

"Molly, it's alright, remember me?" he said.

Molly said nothing for a few seconds, then slowly nodded her head. "And Percy and Harold, yes? Here are your friends?"

"Yep," said Percy, smiling at her. "Percy is my name. Look, we've got some food for yer. Harold here will get it."

Harold took the hint and went to fetch the wooden plate with Molly's meagre portion of bread and cheese and her can of water. She ate quickly, and gulped the water down, draining every drop and then shaking the cup as if to make more materialise.

"Wishing for some more to come? It was like that for us too," said Noah.

She said nothing, just laid her head on Noah's shoulder. Her eyes were wide and red and tired.

"Poor little robin," whispered Harold. "She's nowt much bigger than our Ellen at home."

"Ellen? Is that yer sister?" Percy whispered back.

"Yep."

No one spoke for a good few minutes after that. Only the sounds of the countryside flitted into the silence now and then, soon joined by Molly's gentle sighing as she once again fell asleep. Soon that was joined by a deluge of dry throaty snores from three exhausted boys. The summer sun began to cool. Night-time pulled a dark curtain across the sky. The moon began its watch…

Noah was back at the river. Beams of honey-coloured moonlight bounced on the water, which lapped gently over small stones and rocks before creeping into darker places then speeding up and flowing away. As he watched, he was suddenly aware of a man standing next to him, holding his school satchel. He knew it was his because of the small ink stain. He had once spilled some ink on the floor at school and a little had splashed onto the bottom edge of the bag.

Suddenly he knew what was inside.

All the bad things he had ever done were in there.

The man suddenly threw the satchel into the river, and it was gone.

Then he woke up.

Lying there with his eyes wide open, he knew something had changed inside him. He wasn't the same Noah. He didn't want to tell lies any more. He wanted to be honest and… yes, brave. And above all he had to do something to get them all away from this horrible life.

If they stayed there any longer, they would die.

But if they tried to escape it could be risky. What about the dog? It could kill them if it was let loose. He thought about the dog and the more he thought about it he began to wonder.

A dog in a cowshed? Would you really keep a dog in a cowshed? He knew nothing about cows, but surely a dog would scare them, especially if they had calves to look after?

The only way he could find out was to go there and see.

The others were still asleep. Just as well, as they might stop him from going. But he knew he had to do it, so making as little noise as possible he got himself up. To get to the cowshed he had to walk up the field where he had been picking stones, through to the back of the farmhouse then round to the front where the door was.

He set off, trusting the light of the moon that went before him, lighting the way. At least the night was warm, that was something to be thankful for.

A sudden hoot from an owl made his heart beat a bit faster. Stopping to listen for any more sounds, he waited, but all was still and quiet again.

Eventually the back of the farm loomed into view through the darkness. Tiptoeing along, he felt for the wall. He felt his way with one foot along the bottom and then made his way along the back of the farmhouse and then to the back of the attached cowshed.

Another sound. A rustle of something. He stopped still, listened once more. There was nothing; maybe it had just been some night-time animal.

Arriving at the cowshed, he turned the corner and tiptoed round the side, then around the next corner, where he stopped a short way along the front of the building. He breathed a sigh of relief and rested his back against the wall, out of breath, his feet aching.

Now all he had to do was find a door. He knew there were a number of them. Edging his way along the uneven bricks and fumbling for the knotty feel of wood, he stopped when his fingers touched something grainy. There it was.

He found the handle and winced at the creak as he inched it open, holding his breath and standing still for a moment to listen.

There was nothing.

He crept through the doorway. It was very dark, so he waited for a moment until his eyes were used to it. His heart was beating very fast now, his mouth dry. A memory echo of the words Harold had said began to play in his head. *"Didn't he tell yer about the dog? They say it would tear yer to pieces if yer get anywhere near it. He keeps it in t'cowshed."*

It would be so easy to turn back. No one would know… but a little girl's life depended on them getting away, so he took a slow, deep breath to calm himself down and stepped forward, peering through the gloom. He could just make out two rows of open boxes, one on either side of the shed, a passageway running through the middle. Noah guessed this was for feeding. A cow stood unmoving in each box, asleep, he presumed.

He had never been so close to so many cows before. He had never liked cows. They were such big things, even bigger now that there were a number of them so nearby. And big enough to do him harm. Listening all the time for the sound of a bark, he began to creep down the passageway. Suddenly a cow trumped in its sleep, and he stopped still, listening to the silence. Surely a cow trump was loud enough to wake a dog? But there wasn't a sound, only a pong of cow wind.

Surely if there was dog in the cowshed it would have been barking by now?

There was only one thing left to do.

Taking a long deep breath, he lurched himself forward, sprinted to the end of the barn, and crouched down, listening for any sounds of a dog, his whole body on hyper alert. There was nothing except for a sudden low moo from a sleeping cow, its deep notes forlorn. Noah jumped slightly, and then steadied himself.

He dashed back to the entrance and again crouched down, listening.

Nothing.

Not even any cow sounds.

He had run the whole length of the cowshed and back again safely. A sudden surge of anger mixed with relief flooded his body. There was no dog. They had been tricked. The gangmaster had made the dog up to frighten them out of any escape attempts. How cruel was that? To scare children – even little ones like Molly?

He must get back to the others. They had a good chance of escaping now. He knew it had to be now before it got light, before anyone might see them.

Leaving the cowshed was much easier than going in. He simply tiptoed out, closing the door softly behind him, listening out for any noise at all. When he got back to the field, everyone was still asleep. He crouched down and nudged Percy gently in the ribs. He had to ask him for permission for something he might find difficult before he woke the others up. "Percy! Wake up. You have to wake up. It's important."

Percy mumbled something in his sleep and rolled over.

Noah shook him again, with a little more force this time. It did the trick. Percy shot up bolt upright then started murmuring some unintelligible words, his eyes wide and staring. Noah thought he made out the words "Tell me the answer, boy," among the rest.

He nudged him again. "Percy… it's me. Noah. It's just a dream. You're not at school now."

Percy groaned, rubbing his eyes. "Noah? Thank goodness… I were just back at school in t'workhouse…"

"Do you remember where you are now?"

Percy did not reply straight away. He scratched his chin, frowning up at the open sky. "Oh aye," he said eventually. "It's come back to me. I'm on someone's farm. What yer wake me up for? I need me sleep."

"Sorry, but I had to."

Noah told him what he had just done.

Percy stared at him. "An yer went in t'cowshed? Yer could have got yerself torn to bits."

"That's why I didn't wake you. I had to do it myself."

"It were a brave thing to do, but—"

"Never mind that. It means we can escape now, there's a chance we can get away. But it has to be now, while it's dark."

Percy nodded. "Oh, I get it, before they all come back in t'morning."

"Yes. And… and there's something I have to ask you before I wake the others."

"What?"

"I know you want to find a new home… but there's Molly."

"Molly?"

"Yes. We have to take her home before we look for the river. She might have a mother and father looking for her."

No reply.

"Percy… did you hear me?"

"Yer right, I know, only…" Percy's voice faded out, thin and small.

"I know. But afterwards we can look for the river. Harold can come with us, too, his home sounds pretty bad to me. Shall I wake him up?"

Percy nodded. "Aye. Let's do it."

Chapter Eleven

Unlike Percy, Harold woke immediately. Noah filled him in on the non-existent dog and the plan to take Molly home. "And we'd like you to come with us," he said, finishing his tale. "To look for this new home Percy is searching for."

Harold blinked at him. "Yer want me with you?"

Noah nodded.

Harold smiled a tiny smile, and then looked back at Noah. "Yer were so brave, doin' that." He sneezed, wiping his nose with a handful of grass. "An' there's only you folk in t'whole world I'd want to stay with. Ma don't love me, and Pa's gone off."

"So it's agreed?" asked Noah. "Take Molly home first. Then us three look for the river."

"Yep," said Harold and Percy together.

"Then I'll wake Molly up. I'll try not to frighten her."

"Try tickling her nose with a bit of grass," said Harold.

Noah plucked some blades of grass and shuffled over to her. She was deep in sleep. He tried tickling the end of her nose, but nothing happened. "It's not working."

"Oh, in that case you'll have t'blow in her ear. It won't hurt, it never harmed our Ellen. She woke up every time."

Noah didn't like the thought of that, so he tickled her ear with the grass instead, and this time it worked. Molly moved her head. "It's alright," whispered Noah. "We're taking you home."

Molly gave a little cry.

"Can you remember where you are?"

He knew by her quick breathing she was awake, but she said nothing and kept her eyes tightly squeezed shut.

"Molly, we're taking you home," he repeated. "Can you tell us where you live?"

She mumbled something, but it was too low to catch every word. Noah turned back to Harold and Percy. "She lives in Kettle Bridge. I think that was what she said."

"Aw no, it's Castle Bridge," said Harold. "Lived there once mesen. But us will have t'travel over fields as t'road is too dangerous, us might be seen."

"Right. Let's do it. And quickly," said Noah. "There's a bit of light from the moon to see by."

"'Appen Molly has gone back t'sleep," said Percy. "She's makin' little snorts."

Noah sighed. "We'll have to piggyback her anyway. Maybe we can pick her up without waking her."

"I'll do it," said Harold. "I've given our Ellen lots of 'em. I'll go first. I can find my way to that road with me eyes closed. You follow behind and listen out for anything."

Harold bent down with his back to Molly and scooped her up gently, shifting her tiny body weight onto his back. He took hold of her legs and arms and wrapped them round his body and neck. Noah watched in awe – he made it look so easy. She didn't even wake up.

"Right. Follow me," Harold whispered. "Stay bending down like me, an' do what I does."

Without making a sound they began to follow him, creeping their way along the hedge. Then, reaching the end of it, they turned towards the farm. The moon helped by spilling out a pale light, enough to just about see the back of one other as they shuffled along. But the farmhouse ahead of them was in shadow, giving it an unearthly ghost-like presence. Thankfully there was no sound from Molly.

Harold stopped as they approached the house. "We have to get ourselves round t'front to get t'road," he whispered softly, "so us must be as silent as t'grave. If yer hear anything, lie down."

Keeping a fair way from the farmhouse and the cowshed, Harold led them in a wide semi-circle around the front of the farmhouse. Noah, having already made one journey that night, was now feeling very tired, but he kept on going, willing his feet to make each weary step. Surrounding trees hovered like ghostly giants waiting to be woken up, rustling their branches in the gentle night-time breeze. Noah felt very small as he crept through their shifting shadows.

He sensed rather than saw the road. His feet, now stumbling on stones instead of grass, told him they were now on the road that he and Percy had arrived on… was it only the day before? It seemed longer than that.

Harold came to a sudden halt and sank down, leaning to the side to slide Molly over to a raised bit of bank by the edge of the road. She shifted in her sleep and moaned a little. Harold, gasping for breath, whispered, "Us need to get us breath back."

Noah managed an exhausted "yes" as he slumped down with Percy, who simply breathed out a long deep sigh.

Noah closed his eyes. How he longed for sleep.

Harold's sudden voice snapped Noah's eyes open. He had nearly drifted off. "Look at Molly." A little shaft of moonlight was lighting up her face, showing her thumb resting against her mouth. Her eyes were firmly closed.

"Not a flicker," said Noah. "Not woken up at all."

"Nope," whispered Harold. "Just as well – us 'ave a long way to go yet. We'll rest up a few minutes then we'll have to get down t'road an away across a couple of fields to be on t'safe side. Then us can rest up a bit an' get a bit of kip."

"That sounds a good plan," said Noah.

Percy didn't say anything, the only sounds from his direction the occasional snore.

"We mustn't let him sleep too long," said Harold a few minutes later. "Us might drop off too, an' bet yer 'orses it's daylight… an' that's us caught for good."

"Yes," Noah said. "Too dangerous to stay. I'll wake him then we'll go. I'll piggyback Molly this time."

"Thanks."

Noah nudged Percy gently in the ribs. "Percy, wake up! Sorry, but we must keep moving."

Percy jumped a little and opened his eyes. "Must've drifted off."

"Time to go." Noah gently lifted Molly, copying the way Harold had wrapped her round his back, and she somehow stayed sleeping with only the occasional murmur and snuffle.

Molly was heavy on Noah's back. He forced himself to move, one foot in front of the other, eyes pinned on Harold ahead of him. There was still enough moonlight to see a little way ahead. They crept slowly down the road where the gangmaster had brought Noah and Percy in the horse and cart, then quickened up their pace as they came to the bridge. Now they were out in the open, no trees to hide them. Noah was on full alert, looking in all directions, listening out.

Once they had crossed the bridge, walked on further around a right-hand curve, trudged across a field and climbed over a low hedge, Noah was past the stage of exhaustion. He had no idea how he had managed so far. Something – or was it someone? – was helping him. He stood still, leaning forward, gasping.

"Don't sit down, or you'll never get up again," whispered Harold. "One more field to go, then us can stop for a kip."

One more field to go. He simply had to make it that far.

After a few minutes standing to get their breath back, they set off again, following Harold. Noah winced at the pain in his knees from the previous day's work and from creeping bent double to avoid being seen. He was grateful to be able to stand straighter again.

Weaving around clumps of trees, Harold seemed to know where he was, even in the dark. That was a relief for Noah. He was grateful not to have to make any more decisions – just to follow was enough effort in itself. He breathed in deeply. The night air was still warm with only a few noises from nocturnal animals to break up the thick countryside silence.

Eventually they reached a low fence. Harold jumped over it first, then reached his arms out for Molly, and Noah handed her over then scrambled over with Percy close behind. Harold beckoned them to keep following him and walked off to the side of the field.

Stopping suddenly at the edge, Harold said, "Us will be safe now. Us needs to get down this 'ere bit, but steady like, as it goes down a fair lot."

Noah looked down. Even in the dark he could see a sharp dip in the land. It reminded him of the trenches they had in the war. His father had told him that was where the soldiers lived and fought and died too. It sounded horrible.

But this trench was to be their shelter for the night; a welcome rest. The dip was low enough for them not to be seen from the field. Very slowly, feeling tentatively for each step, they made their way down into the trench. Harold carefully lay the still sleeping Molly on a thick patch of grass, then the boys found their own patches nearby.

Noah, very warm from the effort of running, creeping, and carrying the little girl, lay awake for a little while. The summer night was warm, but he cooled down eventually. The sides of the trench made him feel as if he was enclosed in a child's cot. He thought of his mother. She seemed close tonight, and he found himself almost believing in heaven now.

Feeling strangely calm, soothed by a lullaby of night-time whisperings, he soon fell asleep.

It only seemed a few minutes later when he woke up, his ears filled with the happy trills of early morning birdsong. It took only a few seconds to work out where he was. A faint smell of something like cabbage water drifted into his nose, maybe from a nearby plant. Sitting up, he screwed up his nose to stop his mind forming a picture of school liver.

"Noah, yer woken, then?" Percy asked.

"Mmm."

"Harold's still snorin' away over there."

Noah smiled. "What about Molly?"

"Same thing. Not snorin', I mean, just not movin'."

"Not moving… is she alright? I mean…" Noah didn't like to say the word in his head. "I'll go and take a look."

Shuffling across to where she lay, he peered into her face, and relaxed when he noticed her eyelids flickering. "Molly," he said, gently touching her shoulder. She opened her eyes, looked at him then gazed around, wide-eyed. Noah was just about to say lots of soothing things when she suddenly sat up, took a good deep breath, and started clapping with a big grin on her face.

Noah was taken aback, wondering if she had lost her senses. He explained how they had got there and finished by telling her not to worry because they were taking her home.

"Don't want to go home," she said defiantly. "Now that the nasty man has gone, I want to stay here."

Noah, thinking maybe she hadn't understood what he was saying, said it all again.

"No. I won't go. I want to stay here and never go home."

Noah was taken aback for the second time and did not know what to say. He had expected her to be frightened, like when he first met her. But now she was so very different.

"Ma never lets me out," Molly said. "I have to stay indoors and play with dolls and spinning tops and rocking horses and not get dirty. Ma makes me wash my hands lots of times and I mustn't go near windows and doors. I hate her." Her voice gained volume with each word. Then she jumped up, leaving them in stunned silence as she ran over to some bushes and crouched down among them, trying to hide. "I'm not going anywhere!" she shouted.

Noah and Percy simply sat and looked at each other, not knowing what to say or do.

"Stop shoutin'!" Harold's sudden voice broke the silence. He'd woken up, and Noah wasn't surprised. The noise that Molly had made would have woken an army up. "Stop that noise!"

"Harold! Remember where yer are?" asked Percy.

Harold sat up and looked around, rubbing his eyes. "Oh aye. I does now. I thought I were back 'ome with me sister. It were her voice… an' she were shoutin' me t'get up."

"No, it's Molly," Percy said, going on to explain all that had happened.

"I thought her 'ome would be a good one," said Harold.

"Yes, we did too," said Noah.

Percy sighed. "You'd think she would be glad she's got a ma an' a pa."

"Yep," said Harold, giving himself a good stretch. "'Appen us will 'ave to talk to her about it. She 'as to go home. Can't leave her out here any road, it's not right."

Percy scratched his nose, frowning. "Why does she do all that grumbling? Lots of little 'uns would give their arms for some toys to play with. 'Appen she's making it all up. An' slowing us down, an' all. An' stopping me from finding a new home. I'm sick t'back teeth of her."

Noah stared at him. "Never heard you get angry before."

"Me too," said Harold, getting up. "Can't have her spoiling our plan. I mean… she has to come with us or it's t'police, onions an' all."

The three of them made their way over to Molly, who stared silently and defiantly out at them from her perch in the bush. Percy stood and scowled at her, his arms folded across his chest. Noah was wondering where Harold would find a policeman, and wasn't there a danger the gangmaster might see him if he went to look for one? He glanced sideways at Percy, but he was just looking ahead, his face blank. Noah saw him scratch his nose once then his ear. His friend wasn't happy.

"Right then," said Harold, straightening himself to full height. "What's this about yer not going home?"

Noah was surprised at Harold's stern voice. He waited to see if Molly would cry. She didn't. Instead, she stood up, dusted her hands and looked Harold full in the eyes. "You can't make me."

Noah didn't move, waiting for Harold to mention the police, but he didn't. Noah breathed out a sigh of relief, wondering if Harold had met his match in Molly.

Harold shoved his hands in his pockets, looking annoyed. "But yer pa and ma will be looking for yer. An' there's nowt like a good home."

"Ma is a rotten pig," replied Molly, stamping her feet.

Then she told them about how her mother thought that fresh air was bad for her. And how she would sneak outside when her mother had an afternoon nap. She had done that, and was picking some flowers, when the nasty man had come and taken her away. Then she told of her pa who was a doctor and read stories to her and she liked him a lot. After she had finished, she folded her arms.

They stood in stunned silence for a moment.

"Nay, lass," said Harold, leaning forward into the bush and patting her on the head. "Us don't mean any 'arm. You've 'ad it a bit bad. I'm thinking now about what yer said… if yer come with us, yer could pick some flowers an' give 'em to yer ma when yer get 'ome and tell her how t'fresh air made 'em grow nice."

"Oh, how lovely!" said Molly, breaking into a smile. "And then she might let me go out."

"Yep. So are yer comin', then?"

"Yes." She nodded firmly.

"That's a good girl," Noah said, relieved.

Percy was unsmiling and said nothing.

"That's sorted then," said Harold, ignoring Percy. "'Appen right now us need some breakfast."

Noah, noticing that Harold was looking directly at him, suddenly remembered he was the one with the money. He had told them about finding it when he had told them all about himself. Reaching in his pocket, he took out the bag of coins and opened it. Harold peered inside and whooped, slapping his leg. "Tha's got enough money there to buy a bloomin' palace, onions an' all!"

Noah felt sick again at Harold's frequent mention of onions. Why he kept on about them he had no idea. He rubbed his tummy in the hope it would put a nice food picture in his head instead.

"I know a bakery," said Harold, "it's in t'next village, but us all 'ave to run a couple of fields first." Not waiting for an answer, he set off at a pelt. Noah took hold of Molly's hand, helping her out of the bush, and they ran after Harold with Percy dragging behind, still looking glum.

Molly didn't last long running, so Noah picked her up and carried her, trying to keep up with Harold, who stopped after dashing across two big fields. They were all out of breath, so they flopped down on a bank by a shaded stream. The lads made no attempt to speak, all trying to get their breath back. Molly didn't seem at all tired now after her carry from Noah and scampered happily in some long grass.

Noah began to wonder if he had the strength to carry on. He closed his eyes. Hearing now only the whisper of a breeze in the trees and the faint laughter from Molly, he lay back.

"Right. About that breakfast." Harold's sudden booming voice broke into Noah's doze and he snapped his eyes open, his heartbeat speeding up.

"I'm off now t'get us summat to eat," said Harold. "Need some of that money."

Noah slid his hand into his trouser pocket and plucked the money bag out. "How much do you need? Help yourself."

"Ta." Harold grabbed a number of coins. He looked at them for a while then jangled them in his hand. "'Appen I feel like a Lord afternoonified!" he said, looking at Percy.

Noah, taking that to mean something funny, also looked at Percy. But Percy wasn't laughing. He was frowning.

"Reckon he's got the morbs," Harold called out, running off.

Noah had no idea what the morbs were, but guessed it meant the sulks. There was not even a flicker of a smile on Percy's face. "Percy, say something… just one word will do."

"Sorry," Percy muttered, looking down at his feet.

"Sorry for what?" asked Noah.

"Losing my rag with Molly… it's 'cause I'm proper lost now."

"Lost?"

"I was lost at t'river when it all… it all 'appened with t'gangmaster… an losin' the dog. An' now I don't know where I'm…" Percy broke off into a sob.

"Where we're going?" Noah finished for him.

"Yep."

"When we set off it was because you thought the rainbow was pointing to your new home."

"Yep."

"And you said it was a promise from God?" Noah didn't want another "yep", so he carried on. "I'm… well… not the same, now, and it's just… I can't put it into words." Noah felt his face flushing with colour, but he was determined to continue. "So… why don't we say a prayer?"

Percy stared at him, his eyebrows rising in surprise. "Never thought yer would ever say that. Go on, then."

Noah took a deep breath, his pulse pounding at his throat. He began, forgetting to close his eyes. "Um… I mean… please God, can you find Percy a home? Amen."

It was done. Percy said a tearful "Amen" and sniffed, scratching one side of his chin.

Looking down at his feet, Noah wondered what to do next. Was he supposed to wait for a voice telling him what to do?

They sat together in silence. Noah felt a bit awkward and fiddled with a bit of grass.

It was fortunate that not too many minutes passed by before Harold returned, sprinting down the bank carrying a loaf of bread under each arm. Molly, seeing the food, came running over.

Harold stopped, panting. "I got two loaves, an' a pie each."

Noah saw Percy grin, and grinned back. Oh, the relief of things being right once more. Two pies appeared from one of Harold's trouser pockets followed by two from the other pocket. Noah breathed in the fresh meaty smell. This was so much better than school liver! Breakfast at last.

"Oh, it's a real picnic and it's outside!" cried Molly.

"Yes, best place to eat," said Noah, remembering the breakfast he and Percy had eaten by the river.

"No gangmaster then?" asked Harold, flopping down on the grass next to Noah and passing the warm pies around.

"No," said Noah. "No sign of anyone."

"Yer sure?" asked Harold. "'Ave yer looked?"

"No, but…"

"Reckon he's just gone an' got some other nippers to be nasty with."

Noah could only nod his head, as his mouth was full of pie.

They had escaped. He was sure of it.

What could go wrong now?

Chapter Twelve

They ate their breakfast and Noah enjoyed every bite. After they had finished, Harold wandered down to the stream and took a long, slow drink. Percy followed and did the same, cupping his hands in the water again and again. Noah hung back. Molly was busy collecting dandelions.

Harold called out to Noah, "What's t'matter? Yer need a drink."

"Is it alright?"

"What yer mean?"

"Drinking water from a stream?"

"Course it is. Bet yer boots. Us have been drinking it for ever an' never had the ague."

Noah thought about what his father would have to say, but then his father wasn't there to see him, so he threw caution to the wind and ran down to the stream to drink. Molly followed him with a fistful of dandelions which she carefully laid by the water's edge. Then she ran into the stream, jumping in the water and splashing it everywhere. Clearly germs didn't bother her a bit. Noah didn't stop her – why would he? She was having fun. They all sat on the bank and watched her.

After a few minutes of rest Harold got up. "Time to get going."

"I'll piggyback Molly," said Percy, now fully recovered from the morbs.

"Aye, lad, when time comes when t'lass is fair gone, but she ain't now. Let her scamper about with us. Call her up now, us better get going," Harold said.

"Molly! Us have to go," Percy hollered immediately.

"Not so loud," hissed Harold, looking around.

"Molly… us knows tha' likes flowers," Percy said in a quieter voice. "There's some more in t'next field."

He was making it up of course, Noah knew that, but it did the trick. Molly came straight away and they set off together, always walking at the edge of the field close to hedges and trees. Dividing one of the fields from the next one was a stile between a crooked wooden fence. Harold climbed it first and then helped Molly over, and Percy followed.

"I'll catch you all up," Noah called. "Need a wee." Not knowing if they had heard, he ran off towards a large bush.

A few minutes later he set off running back to them. He could see Percy and Harold bending down in the distance, picking something off the ground. He couldn't see Molly anywhere.

"Where's Molly?" he said, catching up to them and holding the stitch in his side.

"Thought she were with you," said Harold, standing up and shading his eyes as he looked around.

"No… I told you I was going to do a wee."

"Oh… blow me 'ead, yer did. Well, 'appen a minute ago she were picking things in t'grass. Me and Percy saw some bilberries, so we stopped to pick some for us to eat. Didn't see her go."

"She can't have gone far," Noah said, ignoring the berries spilling from Harold's and Percy's hands. "She's only got little legs."

"Aye, that she 'as," agreed Percy.

"We'll have to go back and look for her," Noah said, a funny feeling lodging in his stomach. "Come on." He raced back towards the stile and Harold and Percy dashed after him, bilberries flying everywhere.

Noah clambered over the stile and gazed in all directions, scanning what he could see of the field. He could feel his heart speeding up. "She might have fallen somewhere," he called out to the others.

"Yep," panted Harold, jumping the stile in one go. Percy took a little longer getting over.

They stood together, desperately searching the horizon.

Suddenly, Noah started striding forward. He had just seen some patches of long grass further up near to a hedge on the other side of the field. He pointed at them. "See that? That's the most likely place. Reckon she's found some flowers there."

"Aye," replied Harold, setting off after him.

Approaching the long grass, Noah spotted some poppies growing in clumps, their bright red heads swaying slightly in the summer breeze. He suddenly smelt danger. Hadn't his dad said something about poppies? He tried to remember.

ANNE JORDAN

Then it came to him.
There was no time to lose.

Chapter Thirteen

Noah could see the poppies more clearly now. Speeding up, he caught sight of what looked like a heap of clothes showing above some smaller tufts of grass. Hurdling over obstacles in the ground, he raced towards the pile, Percy and Harold a fair bit behind now.

What he saw next made his heart miss a beat.

Lying face down in the grass was Molly.

She wasn't moving. His father had warned him about poppies as they were poisonous. It was the seeds. They contained opium, a dangerous drug. They could make your teeth go yellow. His father had made him promise never to go near them.

"Molly!" he called out. "Molly, are you alright?"

"What did you shout for?" said Molly, suddenly jumping up and scowling at him. "You've frightened them away!"

Noah crouched down beside her, forcing himself to smile, his heart rate slowly dropping. He noticed a little flurry of bugs scuttling along the ground.

Just then Harold and Percy came running up. "What was yer doing, runnin' off like that?" said Harold, kneeling down. "An' not tellin' us, an' giving us a scare! Wait… them flowers are—"

"Not nice," interrupted Noah.

Harold gave Noah a questioning look, and Noah mouthed the words *"don't frighten her."*

Harold nodded, but he wasn't smiling.

Percy started kicking at the poppies.

"Not the pretty flowers! Please, they will die…" cried Molly, her eyes leaking with tears.

"Molly, them flowers are… oh… not nice," said Harold, remembering just in time not to say *poisonous*.

Noah nodded his thanks and then helped Molly to her feet. "Come on now, back over the stile. Then we can look for some prettier ones."

Molly tore her hand away and didn't answer. Her cross face said it all.

They all set off together, a weary group making their way to the stile. None of them jumped over it this time, just climbed slowly over, one by one.

Harold once again took the lead as they trudged on across the field in silence. All Noah could hear was the occasional sniff from Molly, clinging to his back because she was too tired to walk.

Harold stopped next to a gap in a stone wall at the other end separating the field from the next one and leaned against it, crossing his arms. Noah and Percy stopped still, waiting for him to speak. "We 'ave to speed up now, so as to get to where we should've got to," he said. He pointed to the west, way beyond the wall. "See that gap over there? Us 'ave to walk to it. An' then through it, an' through another field, then up a little hill and then us end up at river, got that?"

Noah and Percy both nodded.

"Then we'll stop. But now we 'ave to move ourselves just to be on t'safe side as there ain't no trees till us get right close t'river. There's no other way, onions an' all."

Noah looked at Percy, waiting for him to say something, but he didn't. He couldn't quite work out what Percy was thinking as he had never seen that particular look before. He sighed, knowing it was now up to him to say something. "We have to, you're right. You know the way. We don't."

"Right then, 'appen we should be off," said Harold. "Us can take turns piggybacking Molly."

Noah carefully helped Molly down and without a word Percy took over, heaving her onto his back. Harold walked off faster than before, leading them out towards the west. After another field, he stopped to take Molly from Percy.

On the way Noah looked once or twice at Percy but he didn't speak. Noah still couldn't make out what his friend was thinking. It was puzzling.

It was only a little hill when they got there, but Noah, already tired out from everything earlier, was now beyond exhausted. His legs ached so much he wondered how much more he could take. How Harold was keeping going he had no idea.

Just as he thought he could not move his legs one more step they arrived at the top of the hill. Noah saw the river stretching out ahead, with its arched stone bridge set into the bank on the other side. "We're here," he breathed, slumping to the ground.

Percy smiled a little as he helped Molly down onto the grass.

After only a couple of minutes rest, they started up again, racing down the hill together. Noah slipped over twice but he didn't care. All he could see was the crystal clear sight of a Yorkshire river burbling and trickling and beckoning them closer.

The river was very low, the muddy bed showing in patches. Large moss-covered boulders cuddled up amidst the flow of water reflecting wide blue skies and white clouds. Taking their shoes off, they all sat down on the bank and bathed their sore and blistered feet. For Noah and Percy this was the second time they had bathed their feet in cool river water. It was pure joy.

After a few minutes they rubbed their feet dry with clumps of grass then lay back on the grassy bank, the warm summer air floating over them. Eyes began to close, but Noah fought to keep his open, fascinated with a robin flying between some trees nearby. How could such a small bird be so swift and strong? He was surprised to see it as he thought they were only around in winter. But eventually even a robin couldn't stop him from dozing off.

A few minutes later he woke. Had he heard something? He listened. Yes. There it was, a faint sound of a human voice… and it was getting louder.

He lay quite still, hoping he had imagined it. No. There was a voice – he could definitely hear it. But it didn't sound like a man's voice. Could it be a child? Maybe one who was lost or escaping from something… someone just like them?

Rolling over to Harold, he gently prodded him in his side. Harold opened his eyes and sat up immediately. "Must've dropped off."

Noah placed two fingers over his lips. "Hush… not too loud. I thought I heard a voice just now… but I don't think it's a man's."

"Where?" asked Harold, glancing around.

"Behind those trees at the top of the bank."

"In t'field?"

"Yes."

"Right. Look, you stay put, an' if t'others wake up, keep 'em from talkin. I'll creep up t'hill and 'ave a look."

Noah watched whilst Harold crept carefully up the hill. He waited, almost holding his breath.

A few minutes later Harold returned, out of breath. "It's alreet, it's just two grand ladies havin' a picnic."

"What do we do?" whispered Noah.

"Hungry, are yer?" asked Harold.

"Yes… but we can't steal their food!"

"Who said anything about stealin'?" Harold winked at him.

Noah couldn't think of an answer so he simply said nothing.

"Look. We just tell 'em us are lost getting home an' we've no food," Harold continued, his voice speeding up.

Noah didn't answer. He felt bad about the idea of lying, now. How he had changed from just the day before!

"Hey, it's not like us are not tellin' t'truth. 'Appen we're all lost from us homes, anyway!"

Noah couldn't argue with that. He had no idea how they would get back to their bit of river when they'd got Molly home and the time came, so he just nodded.

"Right then. Wake Percy, but not Molly. Let her sleep. I 'ave a plan."

Chapter Fourteen

Noah looked at Percy, wondering what he was thinking. Harold had just told both of them his plan to carry a sleeping Molly up the hill so that the grand ladies would see them. The idea was to say they had lost their way and Molly had fainted with hunger. "I'll do all the talkin'," Harold finished.

Percy said nothing. Grabbing a handful of grass and wrenching it out of the soil, he threw it as hard as he could down the hill. Noah could see he wasn't happy.

He didn't feel too good about the idea himself.

"Look 'ere," Harold began, but then stopped at the sound of Molly murmuring in her sleep. He beckoned them further up the hill, away from her. "Yer 'ungry, ain't yer, both of yer?" Not waiting for an answer, he went on. "Us need to eat to keep going or us will start fainting away. An' worse too… folk die from no grub."

Noah thought Harold was being a bit dramatic, especially the bit about dying. But they did have to eat, he was right about that. "Alright," he said eventually, but even he could hear the flatness in his voice.

"Good," said Harold. He turned to Percy. "What's yer thinking?"

Percy gave him a sour stare.

"Don't look so accusing. Say summat! It's for yer own good."

"Aye. S'pose so," Percy said finally, scratching his nose frantically. "But we 'ave to get going straight after."

Noah felt sad to see Percy scratching such a lot. He hadn't done that for a while.

"Yep. Course us will. No messin' about. Right… I'll get Molly, an' I'll go in front. You follow behind an' act like yer goin' t'die any minute. Rub yer belly an' groan an' so on."

Harold crept towards the still sleeping Molly and crouched down, then gently slipped his hands underneath her, picking her up with ease and holding her firmly as he got to his feet. It was brilliantly done, and Noah couldn't help but admire his ability to move so well.

They climbed the hill slowly, Molly still slumbering in Harold's arms. A short distance from the top, Harold began to make a strange wailing sound and picked up his pace as he made his way towards a gap in the trees. Noah and Percy followed, reluctantly.

"Who is there?" a posh voice asked, followed by another voice, shaky and high.

"It's not a ghost, is it, Lilian? Please say it isn't. If I see it I'll scream! I can't look."

"Have mercy on us poor lost souls. We're fit to die!" Harold called out mournfully. Molly stirred a little.

Harold gave Percy and Noah a hard stare, and they began groaning and rubbing their stomachs. Noah felt uncomfortable and guessed Percy did too.

As they emerged from the trees, Noah stopped. Sitting down on a blanket a little way from an open picnic basket was a young woman, her jet-black hair caught up in a low bun peeping out from her straw bonnet. She wore a pure white dress with a blue sash around her waist and she looked bewitching.

The other young woman wore a pale green dress and a bonnet, her brown hair tumbling down her neck in ringlets. She scrambled to her feet. "Alexandra, sister dear, you must stop your silliness! These children need our help."

She gently took Molly from Harold and laid her on the picnic blanket. Molly's eyelids flickered, and Noah wondered if she was really awake and playing along.

"Oh, kind lady, us little sister is nigh on dead," moaned Harold.

Just then Molly opened her eyes. Spotting the picnic basket, she sprang to her feet and peered in, eyes wide and smiley.

"Oh bless me socks," Harold said, "it must've been t'smell of food. It's made her better."

The jet-black hair lady began to laugh. It was a strange laugh, starting with a slight cackle then slowing down to something deeper and more refined. Noah thought it a bit odd but then wondered if it was just a summer cold.

"That was a sudden recovery," the ringlet lady said suspiciously. "But sick or not, you all look as if you need feeding up. Cook always packs far too much for us to eat. And it is our Christian and our bounden duty that we should feed the hungry. It is like… I mean, it is in the Holy Bible."

"Oh, kind lady, tha' be a—" Harold had no time to finish what he was about to say. The proud lady was now busy rummaging through the picnic basket.

"Come, Alexandra, sister dearest, help me spread the food and cutlery on the blanket. We must make sure that these children have plenty to eat."

"Yes, Lilian, sister dear. We must feed the little children."

Noah was very taken with the way they talked to each other. He wondered if all Victorian ladies talked like that.

Soon the picnic blanket was filled with attractive plates, cups and cutlery. The food came next. Thick cheese sandwiches made with white bread. Plates of cold meats, roast beef, roast lamb, roast duck. Round, succulent meat pies came next, followed by bowls of fresh apples and pears. A selection of sweet things came after that. Noah liked the look of the jam puffs and fruit turnovers the best. Then bottles of pale yellow homemade lemonade were poured into jugs.

Lilian said grace, and the picnic begun.

About half an hour later, Noah, Percy and Harold were sitting on the bank near the river, dangling their feet in the water and feeling very full up indeed. They had been sent to play whilst Lilian and Alexandra were teaching Molly how to make a straw hat.

"Some picnic, weren't it?" said Harold. "Eee, but me belly is full of oni—"

"Yep," interrupted Percy, giving Noah a knowing look. "Me too, those jam puffs!"

Harold suddenly cried out and held his belly. "Oh no, lads… get out me way." He bolted towards a clump of trees.

Not long after that Noah began to get tummy pains too. He jumped up, his stomach cramping, then ran off in a different direction, leaving Percy all on his own.

When Noah came back, Percy had gone too. He guessed it was the meat that had done it. They'd all eaten too much of it. He had seen Percy put at least four slices on his plate – not to mention a number of meat pies. He slouched on the grass, waiting for them both to come back. He didn't have to wait long before he saw the bent over figure of Harold trudging his way out of the trees.

"My belly ain't 'alf hurtin'," he said, flopping down next to Noah.

"Me too," said Noah.

"Have you been…?"

"Yes," said Noah, not wanting to hear the word. "I never want to see a jam puff again."

"An' Percy?"

"Expect so."

"Yer can blame me if yer want," said Harold.

"No, I'm not blaming you," said Noah. "It was just all that amazing food."

They lay there on their backs, looking up at the sky. Noah's stomach still churned and he pressed his hand against it.

"S'pose Molly is still makin' that bloomin' hat," said Harold, breaking up the silence.

Noah shrugged his shoulders. He didn't care about hats. If this was death it was best if it happened quickly.

"Percy's takin' his time, ain't he? Hope he's alright."

Noah suddenly realised how long Percy had been gone. He dragged himself up and wandered around, up and down the hill, through the trees, trying to spot Percy. He searched in the direction he thought Percy must have gone, but there was no sign of him at all. He went to ask Molly and the ladies, but they'd not seen him either.

He rushed back to Harold, who was still slumped out on the grass. "Percy's gone! Can't find him anywhere."

"What, yer sure?"

"Yes, I looked everywhere."

Harold shrugged. "Well he's had the morbs for ages, reckon he's given up waitin' an' tried to get back down to that bit of t'river he wanted to get to."

"But he doesn't know the way back. What do I do? Stay here or go after him?"

Just then Molly came running down the hill carrying a straw hat, a look of happiness lighting up her face. Noah could tell that she hadn't been sick, but then she hadn't eaten as much as them. "The ladies are gone now, an' I have made this hat for Mother," she said, holding the hat up for them to admire. "An' now I'm going to jump in the river. Catch me if you can!"

Flinging the hat on the ground and charging towards the river, she whooped with joy. Her tiny but very nimble body moved so quickly she took them by surprise. Noah sprinted after her but was too late to stop her from jumping in. "Molly, come out of there!"

Molly ignored him and splashed around, shrieking with delight and wading further into the river, not caring about where she was heading. She clapped her hands in the air and vaulted over some boulders, darting further and further away. Noah ran straight into the river, not even stopping to remove his shoes. She was getting too near some very jagged rocks.

But it was too late. She caught her foot trying to jump over a craggy boulder and went sprawling over, landing awkwardly, her legs sticking out of the water.

"Molly! Oh no, Molly… don't move," Noah called out.

She started to cry, clutching her foot.

"Keep still," Noah said, splashing towards her and crouching down.

"Don't tell me off," she whispered.

"Now, don't get upset. What hurts the most?"

"My foot."

"Nothing else?"

"My hand's bleeding."

"Nothing else hurts, you sure?"

"No, it's my foot," she replied between sobs.

Harold waded up to them. "We'll lift her up together."

Slowly and carefully they lifted her out of the water, then, watching where they placed their feet, carried her out of the river. Noah gently rested her on the riverbank and slipped off her wet shoes and socks. Her left foot had already begun to swell. She would not be able to walk at all. She would have to be carried all the way home.

"Is it far to go now?" he said to Harold.

"No," replied Harold. "Just two more fields then us three can rest up."

"Who do you mean by us three?"

"Just us, yer an' me an' Molly, of course."

"But Percy hasn't come back. Supposing he is trying to find his way back to the river and has got lost?"

"Are yer that bothered? I mean… he left yer. Maybe all that story about being in t'workhouse were just made up. Maybe he's in cahoots with t'gangmaster an' he's out with him getting other kids to work on t'farm. Bit of money in it for him."

"No, it can't be, not Percy! He was crying when I first saw him, and he really wants a new home."

Harold shrugged. "Up to you, mate, but I reckon he's laughing his 'ead off now."

It just didn't make sense. What was he to do? Go and find Percy or stay with Harold and help take Molly home?

His heart was thumping inside his chest.

He felt sick again. Sinking down, he pressed his hands over his eyes to block out the tears that were beginning to fall. Molly mustn't see him upset.

Chapter Fifteen

"Well, are yer coming then, or not?" asked Harold a few seconds later. "Us need to get going."

Harold's voice sounded sharper than usual and Noah was startled. He rubbed the tears away roughly and scrambled to his feet. "But what about Percy?"

"'Appen he's gone for good. Reckon he's off his chump, any road, talking about followin' rainbows."

Noah couldn't believe that. Had he been taken in all this time? It was unbelievable that his friend Percy was mad.

Harold folded his arms impatiently. "What are yer waiting for? We need to take Molly home. That ankle looks really bad."

Harold was right. Noah had no choice. He had to help Harold get Molly home. What to do after that, he really had no idea. He looked at Molly who was lying still and whimpering to herself, her tear-stained face white. No time to lose. He bent down and scooped her up in his arms. She lay there quietly, gazing into his face, and his resolve strengthened. He had to get her home.

"Right then," said Harold. "We take it in turns up t'hill an' across two more fields, then we should see t'village. Us can be there in t'next hour or two."

They set off together, Harold a little way in front leading the way. It was exhausting for Noah having to carry Molly, but he kept his eyes on the ground in front of him and kept going. Molly was silent now, all the fun in her face faded away.

At the top of the first field they swapped over.

After a while, Noah noticed that now and then Harold's legs began to give way. Each time it happened he straightened up again. "Do you want me to carry Molly?" Noah called out after seeing Harold about to crumple to the ground yet again.

"Aye. Being sick an' all's fair worn me feet out. Give us a minute, will yer?" Harold crouched down, gently laying Molly on the grass, and then sank his head onto his knees.

Noah knelt down next to them and waited for Harold to get his breath back.

Harold straightened up a few minutes later. "Aye, that'll do now."

Noah shook his head. "Sit down for a few minutes longer. Don't want you fainting away."

"Oh… right. Yes. S'pose yer right," Harold answered, looking relieved.

They sat in silence, both of them gazing into the distance, Molly lying quietly on the grass with a little whimper now and then.

"Oh… what's that?" said Harold, a few minutes later. "Over there? Just spotted summat… looks like a cottage, I think."

Noah looked in the direction Harold was pointing. "Where?"

"Just next to them big trees that are scraping t'sky."

"Oh yes! I can see it now."

"'Appen there might be folk there who might 'elp Molly. Reckon us should try to get to it."

"It's worth a try," replied Noah, getting up and dusting off his hands. "Help me get Molly on my back. I think I can just make it."

It took all of Noah's energy to get through the last bit of walking, Molly seeming heavier than ever as she clung to his back, but eventually they reached the cottage. It was a strange looking building with no upstairs and the windows bricked up. There had once been a path to the front door, but it was now covered with weeds.

"Don't think anyone lives here, do you?"

"Maybe not," said Harold, "but shall us just go in an' have a look?"

Harold was down the path before Noah had time to answer, pushing open the door which squeaked in protest. "What yer waiting for?" he shouted back at Noah. "Us might get a drink of water if nothing else."

Noah was so thirsty his tongue was nearly sticking to the top of his mouth. He was desperate for a drink, so he followed Harold inside, bending low through the doorway to stop Molly hitting her head.

It was dark but not pitch black. Here and there, tiny shafts of daylight stole in between cracks in the walls. A heavy damp smell hung in the air like a world of wet socks drying by a tiny fire. It was clear that no one had lived there for a long time.

"Not much to stop for," Noah said, turning to go.

"Nah, but 'appen if us 'ave a good look around, there might be a tap somewhere," Harold replied.

"Alright… but if not, we'll go." Noah laid Molly carefully down on the earthen floor and stood up, stretching. He started to inspect the room, bending his head down low to see if there could be any taps near the ground and searching the walls. Nothing. And why had it gone so quiet? He couldn't see Harold… he must be searching the other side of the house, away in the shadows.

He was beginning to feel afraid. There was something wrong here.

Something evil.

Something or someone behind him, a presence of some sort. Was this cottage haunted? He stood up straight, not daring to move. A strange smell, almost sweet, wafted towards his nose.

Then suddenly there were two strong arms grabbing hold of him and yanking him backwards. Molly began to scream.

Somebody was saying something.

It was a voice Noah knew too well.

Chapter Sixteen

"Want to hear a good yarn? Sit down an' I'll tell it yer."

Noah felt the grip on his arms loosen, and he whirled around, trying to make out the face in the shadows. The face he'd never wanted to see again. The gangmaster himself, his face too real, too large, too ugly, even in the darkness.

They had been caught.

Noah spotted Harold, standing frozen near the doorway. "Quick, Harold, there's a chance for you. Go, save yourself!"

Harold didn't move.

"Go now," Noah shouted.

Nothing.

The gangmaster leered closer to Noah, then grabbed his face, pinching his jaw hard and beginning to laugh. Noah saw his teeth, broken and yellow, lit by a shaft of light puncturing a crack in the wall.

Harold snapped out of his trance. He was going to go. Thank goodness at least one of them would get away. Noah breathed a sigh of relief.

But instead of making for the door, Harold came and stood next to the gangmaster. "What yer think, Pa? Got 'em here reet good for yer."

Harold began to laugh, a wide open-mouthed mocking cackle. Noah felt sick.

He knew he had been tricked.

That's when he noticed that Harold's teeth were identical to the gangmaster's. Yellow and crooked.

The gangmaster and Harold were father and son.

"Got it now, 'ave yer? There's more to come, plenty of time for this yarn. An' don't try to escape, or that kid gets the back of me hand." The gangmaster raised his hand threateningly in Molly's direction.

Letting go of Noah's face, he shoved him to the ground, grinning at Harold. "Yer did well, lad. Shall us tell 'im rest of it?"

Harold smirked. "Aye, Pa, tell 'im how well yer lad did."

For Noah, the sudden realisation he had been betrayed cut into his heart. He had no choice now but to stay and listen. Trying to escape was useless. He sat up gingerly, his jaw aching and his stomach clenching, and rested his back against the wall. He tried to give Molly a reassuring look, but she was lying still, eyes shut tight.

"So," began the gangmaster, "I did a bit of stealin', an' I decided to lie low for a bit so as not to be suspected. So I buried t'loot by t'river an' I left it there. Let a few days go by an' waited for fuss to die down. An' when I think right time's come I goes reet early morning to get it. An' when I gets there… it's gone."

The gangmaster spat on the floor and wiped his hand across his ugly, sneery, dribbling mouth.

"So I hangs around a bit an' I sees you an' yer mate. I thinks – has one of 'em found it? So I gets back to Harold an' I tells him me plan of nabbing both of yer, making sure I tells yer about t'dog. All I had to do next was kidnap t'girl. We knew one of yer would see through t'bit about t'dog in cowshed, all us had to do was wait until yer decided to escape. An'…" The gangmaster broke off, settling his steely gaze on Molly then starting to laugh.

"…Guess what? We knew yer both'd want to take the little lady 'ome very upright, just like little gentleman would do."

Reaching down to pat Noah on the back, the gangmaster bowed to him. Then he laughed again, throwing his head right back and showing off his teeth in their full repulsiveness. "Now this is best bit. All me lad 'ere had to do were make sure yer came the long way round. Aye, that's a laugh. T'road would've got yer there in minutes. On t'long way round you'd get hungry an' need to buy some food. So yer takes t'money out of yer pocket an' all Harold 'as to do is run to bakery. An' I meets 'im there, an' he tells me it's you that 'as t'money. No good takin' it then – we 'ad to get yer trapped in 'ere so yer can't go blabbing t'police an yer—"

Stopping mid-sentence, the gangmaster turned his head to the door. "Who's there? I heard summat."

"What, Pa?" Harold said.

"Don't just sit there… get yersen out an' look."

Harold left, leaving a toxic hush behind him.

How Noah wanted to shout for help. How he prayed for help. If only he could dash across and get Molly and make a run for it. But he knew he hadn't a chance. He would be caught before he got to the door.

Oh, if only there was someone who could help. But who? No one could know they were there. It was a cleverly thought-out plan and he had fallen for it.

Harold slunk back in a moment later, saying he had looked around but there was no one there.

"Reet then. Good. I'll finish me story. I missed out funniest bit. Them so posh ladies Flossie and Bassie do best acting in Yorkshire. You should see 'em on stage. Harold's aunties them are, an' as good at stealin' as me. Nay problem getting a picnic basket. An' then Harold does his best bit of acting ever."

Harold beamed. "Ta, Pa."

"That slowed yer down reet well, an' made yer sick. Aye, I saw yer, an' me boy Harold too, well he can take it. Doesn't mind a belting an' sickness if there's a share in t'loot."

Harold smirked. "Aye. An' then the kid helped by hurtin' her ankle. Slowed us down more."

The gangmaster smiled. "So all I needs now is what's mine. Get it, Harold me lad."

Harold strutted over to Noah and shoved his hand into his right trouser pocket. He grabbed the bag of money and handed it to the gangmaster. Noah kicked him in the legs, but knew it wouldn't stop him, and it didn't. It just earned him a harder kick back.

The gangmaster sniggered. "Pity he's such a good little boy. He'd make a good basher. He can think about that when we're gone an' the rats start nibbling."

"Aye, Pa, he could that, onions an' all."

Rats? Noah felt his heart speeding up. "One thing," he said bravely, trying to delay things. "Why all this trouble? Why not just get the money off me when you caught me the first time? Or at the farm? Why bring Molly into it?"

The gangmaster grinned at him. "Had to be sure it was you. And it gave my lad here a good test, leading yer all a merry dance like that. An' we had to bring Molly in to make sure you'd come this way."

Harold started to laugh. "Aye. An' it was fun, too, them lot just followin' me everywhere like that."

"So all that about your brothers dying… all lies?" Noah said.

Harold just sneered.

"Reet then, me lad." The gangmaster reached into his pocket and fished out a key. "Horse is waiting to carry us off to happyland."

Then, with another mock bow from them both, they walked to the door. Harold waved to Noah. "Lovely to make yer acquaintance." He grinned his foulest yellow grin yet then followed his father through the doorway.

The last sound Noah heard was the thud of the thick wooden door then the thin metal clank of the lock, the echoing sound filling the room then dying away, leaving a hollow space thick with fear.

His first thought was for Molly. Crawling over to her, he bent his head near to her face and listened. She had been so quiet all the time they had been in there that he feared something really bad may have happened to her. She was very still. He could hear nothing.

Reaching across, he touched her hand.

It was cold.

"Molly… Molly! Are you alright?"

No answer.

"Molly! Wake up!"

He waited in the heavy silence. Finally, after a few awful seconds, came a faint whimper.

Noah swallowed over the big dry lump in his throat. She was alive. Probably too frightened to speak, but alive. She must have heard it all.

"Molly, if we get out of this together," he whispered, his hand on her shoulder, "I shall buy you the best straw hat ever."

But it was a faint hope. He knew that really.

The truth was that they were trapped. There was no one to save them. Even Percy had gone, the only person he thought of as a friend. Was he laughing at the boy who thought he was from a different time, just like Harold and his father were? Anyone would say he was off his chump.

He had never felt so alone. This was worse than ice-cold baths, worse than school liver, worse than Matron.

Worse than anything in the world except losing his mother.

Dying in an age he didn't belong to in a dismal cottage no one ever visited was his fate now. There would be no grave; after all, it was the 1800s, and he had never been born. There was no Noah Eaton.

Worse still, Molly would die too. He had not saved her.

This was the end.

Trying not to think how long it would take for him to die, he closed his eyes. The sudden complete darkness was horrible, so he opened them again. Only slight fingers of sunlight struggled through the tiny cracks in the walls now; not enough to stop the really bad pictures taking shape in his head.

They always came when he was feeling so bad that life had faded into blackness. And now they came in full colour. He was back at school, a victim of a bully, an older boy named Martin Hakes who wasn't just a bully but a master manipulator, expert at the pretence of being nice when he needed to be. He saw him now, his beady little eyes and his missing tooth, striding towards him and shouting out orders.

Another equally bad picture followed. A science master, not his usual one who told good jokes, but a replacement brought in when he went sick. Noah could see him clearly, small and round with big feet and a voice that hissed as he spoke, standing over Noah at his desk, his cap and gown too big, hissing words like a snake. *"Repeat after me, Eaton:*

'The sun is made of hot gas. The sun is a star not a planet. The sun is the centre of the universe. The sun is made of layers.'" Then again. "Say it, don't stand there muttering."

"Sorry, sir."

"Sorry won't make you a scientist. Application is what you need. Application. Say it, boy."

"Application."

"And again."

"What was that you said... apple?"

No... applic... no, what was it? Oh, yes, *apple*. That was right. A red juicy apple... he could see it now. Oh, to take the first bite... he felt his eyes closing. He was in a garden of apples and—

Bang. Boom. Clang.

Noah's body suddenly jerked awake, his heart racing. Then again. There it was. *Bang. Boom. Clang.* Then again, even louder. *Bang. Boom. Clang.*

Then a creak and a sound like splintering wood. *Crash*.

The door shattering to pieces, bright sunshine flooding in then streaming through his body, a rush of people at the door. A strange man running in, bending over Molly then calling her name, reaching out and touching her face, cradling her to him. Molly crying out "Daddy", sobbing into his chest. The doctor, her very own father. Here.

Then another figure dashing over to him, bending down and touching his shoulder, calling his name. "Noah. Noah! Yer know me, don't yer? Noah, it's me."

Percy?

Could it be? Was it really him? Was the sunshine playing tricks? He studied the face looking at him. A face scarred with scratching. Of course… Percy. He could not believe it. Percy, solid, here with him. Percy, his dear friend. Percy, scruffy, smelling of stale sweat and bad breath, but gloriously real, his red face glowing with relief.

Noah had expected to die. He couldn't speak. His mouth was too dry to make words.

"Yer don't have to say nowt. Must've been reet bad for yer. We've got yer an t'doctor has got his Molly an' we're going back with him, so no botherin', now. Tell yer all about it later."

The wave of relief at seeing his old friend was too much for him. His eyes blurred over and tears of joy cascaded down his face. He didn't care. He was alive. Help had come. Explanations could wait until later. He tried to get up, but his legs buckled under him and he crumpled back onto the floor in a heap.

"Nay bother yersen," said Percy, squatting down next to him. "Stay put. There's help coming."

Noah looked up through a haze of tears. He could just make out a figure, a man, walking towards him.

"Come on, lad. Farmer Ellis, I am, an' I've got an 'orse an' cart waitin' for thee. Aye, an' it knows t'way to doctor's 'ouse."

Strong arms reached down and with no effort at all picked him up and carried him outside. Breathing in the fresh air and praying a silent *thank you*, he was helped up onto a horse and cart.

He was safe, and so was Molly.

Chapter Seventeen

It was late evening. Noah was sitting on a Victorian couch in a small, comfortable parlour in Molly's parents' house. Molly had been put to bed, her ankle bandaged up. It was quiet now after the hullaballoo her mother had made on first seeing her daughter. "I warned her about fresh air," she'd shouted, while hugging Molly tightly to her. "Told her it was dangerous."

Molly's father had listened to Noah's story about the gangmaster and Harold and had then ridden off to find a policeman. Noah and Percy had been given a bath and some fresh clothes to wear, donated by the wife of a neighbour who had helped to rescue them. Molly's mother gave them hot broth and chunks of bread with farmhouse butter, then glasses of hot milk. They felt warm and comfortable and a little sleepy.

With a rug over their knees, they were now ready to listen to each other's story. "So, how did you find me?" Noah said to Percy.

"Yer remember when us were sick? Well, I saw Harold in t'trees, an' he were waving his hands in t'air. He couldn't see me. So I watched. An' he does this thumbs up sign. Then I sees him turn an' come back."

"Reckon he was signalling to the gangmaster?"

"Didn't know what were goin' on, so I decided to watch him. I had no choice but to leave yer with him. Did yer think I'd deserted yer?"

Noah nodded.

Percy lowered his head. "Yep. Sorry. I thought yer might. Anyway… so I hid, but I had to be careful. I heard Molly fall over an' then I heard yer talking an' so I followed yer all, but keepin' low all t'time."

"Didn't see or hear you," said Noah.

"Did plenty of creepin' round in t'workhouse. Any road… 'appen I sees yer going into t'cottage, so I watch an' then I sees t'gangmaster come from t'other direction an' goes in an' then comes out later on with Harold. They were laughing together. I knows it all then. I've seen many a bad 'un in t'workhouse, an' I were always a bit sucipious of Harold."

"Well, I wish I'd been. Got taken in, alright." Noah sighed at the memory of it all.

"It were when us were coming across t'fields. I kept on lookin' out for t'castle."

"What castle?"

"Yer remember when Molly said she lived in Kettle Bridge? Harold said it were wrong and it were called Castle Bridge. So I thought that meant t'village were near a castle, so I kept on lookin' out for it. Nay castle in sight. Molly were right, 'cause t'farmer told me – yer know, him that brought us here."

Noah nodded. "So it was Kettle Bridge."

"Mmm. An another thing… all that picnic stuff. Posh ladies don't talk to us kind except at charity things… an' those nice ones who go t'church."

"And I thought it was you having the morbs," said Noah, now feeling ashamed of himself.

"I were a bit, 'cause it were takin' so long getting anywhere. Any road, back to what I were saying. When I sees that Harold with t'gangmaster, I thinks, what shall I do about that? It were then I sees t'dog."

"A dog? Was it Lolly?"

"Nah. Wish it were. It were barking a lot but it were friendly like. It were like it were wanting me to go with it. So I did. I had a job keepin' up with it, but it stopped till I caught it up. A couple of fields of runnin' an' I was ready to drop but then in t'distance I saw this man on a horse an' he were comin' my way. The dog bounds up to him an'…"

"I think I can guess the rest. It was Molly's father."

"Yep, an' I tells him everything, an' off he goes t'nearest farm an' tells t'farmer – an' t'rest yer know."

Noah told Percy his part of the story. He told him about the fear and the darkness and the relief at the unexpected rescue. "I was just so happy that you hadn't abandoned me after all."

"Us mates, then?" said Percy, his eyes deep with worry.

"You bet I am. You are the best friend I ever had."

Percy beamed. "Aw… good thing. An' about t'rainbow an everything… do yer still want—"

A sudden knock on the door stopped Percy from finishing his sentence. The housekeeper poked her head around the door. "Master Noah, there's someone wanting to see you."

"Me?"

"Yes. She didn't give her name, but she was insistent, so I showed her into the doctor's study."

"Oh. Ah… but I don't know any one round here…" Noah threw the blanket off his knees and followed the housekeeper out of the room. Who could it be? Maybe it was one of the neighbours with some more clothes. He would rather have stayed with Percy. They could have talked some more. There were plans to be made.

The housekeeper led him to the study and showed him in. Standing looking out of the window was a lady, her face covered with a veil. As Noah stepped into the room, she turned, removing her veil and smiling. Noah stared in shock. He knew immediately who she was.

It was the river woman. But why was she here?

"It's time, Noah."

"Time?"

"A true witness delivers souls. Remember? It is now complete."

What was complete? Noah still did not understand.

She answered his thoughts. "You will know very soon. But now it is time to go."

"*No,*" he wanted to shout. He hadn't found a home for Percy. He didn't want to go. He wanted to stay with his friend and grow up in Victorian times. To be around when telephones were invented and cars and aeroplanes and cameras, to work alongside clever engineers and be famous. Not to go back to a cruel boarding school and be a boy who got laughed at.

But when he tried to speak, he couldn't.

The river woman shook her head. "You must go back. It is the only way to know the truth."

She reached out her hand and touched his shoulder. Immediately, a low mist started to swirl around his feet, then spread slowly upwards. Just like the morning he had arrived.

Closer it came, coiling and twirling all around him, enveloping him and drawing him in. He could no longer see his feet. Closing his eyes to stop it happening, he tried to turn back towards the door. But his feet would not move.

He was trapped, returning to a world he no longer belonged to. There was no other choice.

He opened his eyes. The mist had all gone. The morning sun was shining. He was standing alone on the river path at the back of Aunt Margaret's house listening to the low croak of a distant frog, dressed in the clothes he had been wearing then.

Realising he was back where he had started, he began to cry, big salty tears dripping down over his mouth and his chin. He would never see Percy again. Or Molly. Were they now only names on gravestones?

He wanted to go back so very much.

He stumbled back to the bridge and sank down, his back against the wall. This was where it had all begun. He closed his eyes and prayed to go back. Even just to see Percy one more time would be enough.

But when he opened them, everything was the same as before. Cradling his head in his arms, he sobbed, his body aching with grief.

A shadow fell over him and he jumped.

"Noah, you can have one last visit – but that is it."

The river woman! He looked up. She was there in front of him and to his surprise her eyes were full of tears.

"But although you will be able to see other people, they will not see you. This is just a gift, just a glimpse. Then you will return here."

Noah nodded, feeling unable to speak. He tried to get up.

"No, stay where you are, just close your eyes."

He squeezed his eyes tightly shut, hoping that the first person he would see would be Percy. But when he opened them, he was not at the doctor's house.

It was as though he was in a tunnel. He couldn't see very much at all, only slightly in front of him, and he blinked, shaking his head. Gradually, his vision began to clear, and thick walls began to slide into place in front and to the side of him. Two arched windows took their place in the walls opposite each other. Then some benches appeared either side neatly in rows.

To his left, a number of people began to appear. Each one sat down next to one other. At the front, a man wearing a wig appeared and sat down at a raised bench.

Suddenly Noah knew where he was. He was in a courtroom, looking directly at a judge.

Two pale and shadowy figures slowly took form, standing in a box at the side of the judge, one tall, the other much shorter.

Noah could now make out their faces. He recognised them immediately. It was the gangmaster and Harold. The gangmaster stood with his arms folded, staring straight ahead. He had grown a rough beard and his face was thinner. Harold too looked thinner. He gazed up at the ceiling, his lips curling downwards, his body shaking slightly.

They were on trial. Both waiting to hear what would happen to them.

The judge raised his hand. Chattering noises faded away into silence.

Were Percy and Molly and the doctor there? Noah tried to shift his position, to look around, but to his dismay he could only properly see in front of him.

He could only watch and listen as the judge began to speak.

Chapter Eighteen

"Samuel Turner, known to some as The Gangmaster, you are convicted of the theft of the life savings of one Albert Johnson, ironsmith of this parish. On the 19th of July, about nine o'clock at night, you broke into the premises of said Albert Johnson and stole the aforementioned savings."

Mumblings and snorts of shame from the public gallery echoed around the court. The judge held his hand up, ushering them into silence. "Added to this crime," he went on, "is the unlawful kidnap of certain juveniles, also of this parish."

There was a hush in the courtroom.

"You are a man of violence. It has now come to light that working in gangs damages the health of young children. Two of the children you kidnapped were left in a disused cottage to die. If they had done so you would be facing a sentence of murder. You, Samuel Turner, are sentenced to a term of 30 years hard labour in prison. That term begins today."

Noah heard someone call out, "Should be hanged!" Others jeered. Eventually once more there was silence.

"As for you, Harold Turner, you will be sent to a reformatory school for five years. You will be taught a trade to help you find a job once you have left school in the hope that it will stop you from committing a crime again. You will not be allowed to see your father. It may be that being away from his influence you will yet become a decent citizen."

Cries of "Can't see that happening!" and "Should've gone to prison!" boomed through the courtroom. The prisoners were led away, still staring straight ahead.

Noah could hear the sounds of people behind him moving and getting up to leave, but the sounds were getting fainter. Noah wondered if amongst them were Percy and Molly and the doctor and his wife. Oh, how he would have liked to see their faces!

Then, just as the vision came, it all faded away as quickly. Noah closed his eyes as the mist coiled around him, and when he opened them he found himself in the same place as before. He knew then that was all he would ever know. He was back in 1930. The only way he could find out about the Victorian age now would be in history books.

There was no more river woman, just Noah Eaton on his school holidays standing alone by a river.

He didn't feel tired anymore. Just very sad.

What should he do now? He didn't want to go back to the house. That would be too final. He thought for a moment then decided to walk along the path to the place he had first encountered Percy. He knew the exact spot as his mind had taken a photograph of it.

When he reached the place, he stood still and closed his eyes. One by one the pictures began to form, and along with them the voices. Noah sat down right there in the middle of the path, watching and listening.

Standing by the river was a boy whose face was blotched with small red patches, and a white scar that ran down his nose to his top lip. He was wearing rags and shoes with holes that looked like they belonged to a different age.

He didn't speak. He just stared at Noah, his eyes red, his face paling with fright.

Noah heard his own voice saying, "It's alright. I'm not a ghost."

The boy started to back away. Noah heard his own voice again, asking him to stay. "Please. I'm real. I won't hurt you."

A sudden tap on his shoulder blurred the pictures and voices. Opening his eyes, he turned around. It was Aunt Margaret herself, real and solid. "I'm back early. The post has come. There was a letter to me from your father."

Oh no. Were they going to move to a different country? That would mean a different school. That could be bad. More cold baths, more school liver, another school bully. After everything that had happened, he just couldn't take any more.

He opened his mouth to speak but found he couldn't form any words.

"Something wrong?" Aunt Margaret asked, squatting down next to him.

Her kind words broke into his misery. He turned to her and sobbed into her shoulder, his tears dripping down her arm and dampening her skin.

She let him cry, holding him close.

Eventually the torrent subsided until there was just the occasional sniff. Aunt Margaret reached into her handbag and pulled out a handkerchief, offering it to him. He wiped it over his face.

"Want to tell me about it?" she said.

He nodded.

"Take your time."

And so he did. He told her everything, beginning with falling over and finding the treasure. He told her everything that had happened after meeting Percy. He finished with the court trial and his return to the river.

Silence hung between them for a few moments.

"Do you think I'm mad?" Noah said. It was the question he didn't want to ask, but he knew he had to. He searched her face, trying to guess what she was thinking, but she was neither smiling nor frowning.

"No," she said eventually, "you're not mad. I believe every word you say. And I will tell you why. No… better still, I will show you why."

Aunt Margaret got up and began to walk slowly back in the direction of the house. Noah followed, wondering what his aunt was about to show him. How could it be any help?

He took no notice of the bees in the bushes by the steps he had come down earlier. He didn't care whether he got stung or not.

When they arrived at the house, the smell of fresh bread cooking in the oven weaved through the air. It was a smell he usually loved, but today it did not comfort him.

Aunt Margaret walked through the hallway and stopped at a door near to the front of the house. She smiled at Noah. "You didn't see this room yesterday as you were so keen to go into the attic. So I thought it would wait until today. What you are about to see might surprise you."

Noah followed her into the room and stopped short, staring.

What he saw was nothing like anything you would usually expect to see in a house.

ANNE JORDAN

Chapter Nineteen

He was standing in what looked like an old school classroom, tables and chairs lining the walls. At the front was a raised platform with a large desk in front of it. But it was what was above the desk that made him draw in his breath. Inscribed above it in large, old writing was a date: AD 1898. Next to that were the words *'A true witness delivers souls'*.

He could only stand and stare. These were the very words the river woman had said.

"I don't…" his voice trailed away.

"Understand?" Aunt Margaret nodded her head and smiled. "Neither did I, Noah, not until now. But listen – it will become clear. This house was once a school."

"A school?"

"Yes. I bought it at an auction, knowing it would need a lot of modernising. It dated from Victorian times. I got workmen in, but when it came to this room the workmen couldn't come for some reason. Then there was a flu epidemic. It was as though this room wasn't meant to be changed."

"Victorian? So… it was a school when I met Percy?"

"Yes."

"Oh… I've just remembered… when I told him I was staying with you in this house, he said it's a school. So he was right?"

"Yes."

"But I don't understand about the inscription, how come it's here and what does it mean?"

"'*A true witness delivers souls*' is a verse from the book of Proverbs in the Bible. I asked Malcolm, my fiancé – you know, the curate I told you about?"

Noah nodded.

"He said it's to do with rescuing someone. You did that for Percy."

"Rescued him?"

"When he ran away from the workhouse, you promised to go with him to find a new home. It's a bit like when a postman delivers letters and parcels.

In a way you delivered him to a new home. He was safe then."

"But he didn't find one." Noah stared down at his feet.

"Keep listening. It will all make sense. Grab a couple of chairs from over there."

"Where shall I put them?"

"Facing the front for now. There's a reason."

Noah picked up first one school chair then another and set them down facing the inscription. He sat down and read it again, still puzzling over it all.

Aunt Margaret opened the drawer in the desk, and Noah watched as she pulled out a large book and brought it over to him. It looked like a scrapbook. She sat next to him and placed it into his hands. He glanced down at it.

And he gasped.

There on the front cover were the words *'For Noah, the boy who saved me'*.

Underneath the words was a photograph of Percy seated next to Molly, both dressed in smart Victorian clothes. Behind them were the doctor and his wife.

"Percy left this for me...?"

Aunt Margaret smiled. "He must have done."

"But this… and the inscription. I just don't get it… why here?"

"I found it in the desk on the stage. It was covered in a muslin cloth. I took it out and…"

But Noah had stopped listening after the word 'and'. He couldn't help but stare at the picture. Could it mean…? The picture forming in his head was staggering.

"Is what I'm thinking true?" he whispered eventually.

"You mean that the doctor and his wife adopted Percy?"

"Yes." Noah had a great big lump in his throat.

"Turn the pages and find out. Pictures say more than words."

Noah turned the cover page over. Stuck down on the first page was a yellowed newspaper cutting. It showed the doctor and Percy standing by a riverbank, holding up a large trout. Underneath were the words *'Doctor Merrick with his son Percy Shuttleworth who won the fishing competition in…'*

Noah stopped reading, his heart racing, a warm feeling spreading through him. "*Son?* So… the doctor really did adopt Percy."

"Yes," Aunt Margaret replied softly.

"But then why did Percy keep the surname he was born with? Wouldn't he be Percy Merrick?"

"I wondered about that too," said Aunt Margaret. "So I looked it up. Apparently in Percy's time there wasn't a formal adoption process."

"What does that mean?"

"There was no paperwork in those days for things like that, so nothing legal. Anyone could call themselves by anything that they liked. That's even true today. Got it?"

"I think so… so he stayed being Percy Shuttleworth?"

"Yes. And you will see that more later."

Noah stared at his aunt, trying to grasp hold of all she was saying and wondering what she meant by 'later'. All he could grasp for now was that Percy had found a home after all. How wonderful was that?

He looked down at the cutting again, something in the corner of the faded old picture catching his eye. He blinked and bent closer. Wait… was that… could it be?

Just behind Percy, in the corner of the picture, was a dog with floppy ears and a face that was half black and half white. Even through the faded old monochrome image Noah could see that the dog's ears were different shades of colour.

"Lolly!" he gasped.

"Lolly?" his aunt said.

"The dog I told you about… it's Lolly! It is! They found Lolly, Aunt Margaret. They found him and then they kept him, didn't they? Look here." He stabbed his finger at the photo. "Look. He's leaning on Percy with this whole happy dog-grin on his face!"

His aunt smiled. "So he is, Noah. So he is."

Noah felt like his heart was so big with joy it might burst out of his chest.

Just then there was a knock on the door, and in walked Mrs Horner. "Sorry to interrupt, madam. There is a telephone call for you."

Noah gulped. Could it be his father ringing?

"Thank you, Mrs Horner. Probably Malcolm."

Aunt Margaret stood up, gently easing the scrapbook from Noah's hands and laying it on her seat. "Noah, promise me you won't turn around?" she called on her way out.

"I promise," he called back, wondering what she could mean.

He heard the door close gently. He was left alone. Why wasn't he allowed to turn around? Maybe if he just took a little peep over one shoulder? Oh, how he wanted to – and how hard it was to just keep looking in front of him. He tried to keep his gaze on the inscription, but he couldn't quite manage it.

Just one glance. No one would know.

Maybe if he just pushed his chair sideways a bit… or, better still, just turn his head as far as it would go? He began to move his head, just a tiny bit at a time, but then he felt guilty.

Maybe if he just looked out of the window it would take his mind off things.

A few seconds later the sky began to darken. Very soon it grew green-black. Summer birds stopped their chirping as though they knew something was coming. An eerie hush descended. Then little raindrops began to fall, steady at first, then getting heavier.

Now the rain started gushing down in one heavy torrent, then came the violent hailstones, pelting the windows. It was over very soon, the rain dying down to a drizzle. The sky brightened. The sun began to shine. Then a rainbow appeared, clear and radiant.

Had it been only that morning when he had seen a rainbow with Percy? Percy had said it was like a promise. A promise is special.

He would keep his promise to his aunt.

After what seemed an age of waiting, he eventually heard the door open with a creak. Aunt Margaret was here. She picked up the scrapbook and sat down. She had a big grin on her face. "That was a surprise, wasn't it? A summer storm, hailstones as big as pebbles. I thought the windows were going to shatter."

Noah simply replied, "Yes." For him the storm had come at just the right time.

"So then. Let's get back to looking at this scrapbook. Where were we?" Opening the book, Aunt Margaret showed Noah the next page. Noah wanted to ask his aunt about why he hadn't been allowed to look round, but his attention was caught by the picture.

It was a school photo of a class of boys seated with their teacher in the centre. Noah scanned their faces, starting at the top. Seated third on the left on the bottom row was Percy, dressed in Victorian school clothes this time, his hair short and neat. It was him alright, the same scar showing. "It's him."

"Yes – and do you recognise where they are sitting?" Aunt Margaret asked.

Noah looked hard at the photo. "Is it…?"

"Yes. It's outside in my garden. It's not that different from how it is now, is it?"

"Does that mean… no. It's too far for him. I mean…" Noah stumbled over his words.

"Yes, you're right. This is where he came to school. But I left the best bit out – this was a boarding school, so—"

"This was his home!" Noah said excitedly. "He lived here during term time."

"Yes. The doctor must have paid for him to board here. The rainbow you saw with Percy was showing you both of his homes. Think about it – the rainbow arch was curving away from you, but it started right here, at this house."

Noah felt light inside. "So… Percy found not just one home, but two?"

"Yes," said Aunt Margaret. "What do you think to that, then?"

Noah could not answer. Percy, his first true friend, had not only found a home with the kind doctor, but he had lived in a school by the river; not any river, but the one they had talked and laughed by together. The one Noah's aunt's house backed onto.

Noah felt tears prickle the backs of his eyes, and he sank his head into his hands, trying to take it all in.

"Oh, sorry, Noah. It's been some adventure for you, hasn't it? Let's just sit for a bit."

Noah laid his head on Aunt Margaret's shoulder. Sitting in silence together, they listened to the church clock across the road chime midday.

Aunt Margaret patted Noah's shoulder. "Alright now?"

"Yes," he said, sitting up straight.

"There are more photos to see, but I'll skip those and just show you one more for now." Aunt Margaret flipped over several pages. "Look at this one."

Noah looked down at the open page. For a moment he thought she was showing him the one he had just seen, the class photo. But then he realised it wasn't the same children. Noah glanced up at Aunt Margaret and saw that her whole face was shining. "Look at the teacher in the middle," she said.

Percy? It couldn't be! Yet the scar was there. "Is it him?" Noah whispered.

"Yes, it's Percy. He's the teacher."

"You mean that when he grew up he became a teacher here?"

His aunt nodded. "Yes. He must have carried on living here – first as a pupil, then as a pupil teacher, and then as a teacher himself."

Noah could only shake his head. It was getting more thrilling by the minute.

Aunt Margaret closed the book and laid it aside, standing up. "Now… brace yourself for the next bit. You didn't look round when I went out, did you?"

"No."

"Good, because now you can." She took a deep breath. "One… two… three… turn!"

Noah scraped his chair around quickly, but what he saw next was disappointing. He was looking at the back wall and hanging on it were several framed pictures, all in dull colours. He couldn't make out what they were, as a shaft of bright sunshine from a nearby window was paling them.

"Oh," he managed to say, his flat voice echoing back to him.

Aunt Margaret smiled. "Now, don't be disappointed. Come closer and look."

She led him to the first portrait on the left. "Now look… and tell me what you see."

Noah peered at the picture. "It's a man's face… and at the bottom of the picture is a date."

"Right, now. The next one."

Noah looked at the next picture. "A different man with a different date underneath."

This happened twice more. It was getting boring, and Noah had to stop himself from yawning.

"Do you know who they are?" Aunt Margaret asked.

"No."

"I looked them up. They are all past headmasters of this school."

"Oh, are they?" said Noah, trying to sound interested.

"Alright," said Aunt Margaret, laughing. "You don't have to be polite. Now – come and look at this one."

Following his aunt to the last but one picture, he stopped and looked at it, squinting so he could see closer. He stepped back, opening his eyes wide. "No… it can't be. Is that…?"

"Yes! It's Percy. But not as a teacher anymore. He was a headmaster!"

A headmaster? Percy could hardly take it in

"Percy became the headmaster of this school. This was his home until he retired." Aunt Margaret began to clap. "A boy from a workhouse became a headmaster! Think of that."

Noah joined in, clapping his hands hard together. He felt like his chest might explode with joy. Who would have believed it? The boy who was no good at school had become a teacher and then a headmaster! "He carried on living here?"

"Yes," replied Aunt Margaret.

"So… he put the sign up, then?"

"I expect he did. 1898 would have made him about 40, so he could have been the headmaster by then."

"*A true witness delivers souls.*" Noah whispered the words as if he was saying a prayer.

"Yes. Very special. He knew that you would be coming here on holiday in 1930. It was his way of saying thank you, along with the scrapbook."

Noah stood still, staring at the portrait and letting the image fill his mind. This was a picture he would never forget.

But what about now? His friend would be an old man. He'd most likely have died by now. Did he dare ask? Maybe his aunt wouldn't know. He turned to her and took a deep breath. "Aunt Margaret… please, I must know… when did he die?"

His aunt put her hand on his arm. "Now. Brace yourself, Noah. Percy isn't dead. He's alive – truly, he is. He lives in a care home not far from here. Malcolm told me on the phone when I asked him if he knew a Percy Shuttleworth. Malcolm said he often talks to him when he does his visits. I asked him to pop across and invite Percy for lunch."

Noah just stared at her.

"I know it's a lot to take in. But he is alive – in his seventies now. And in about half an hour, hopefully, you will meet him."

Could it be true? Was he really going to see his friend?

Suddenly a dark cloud rushed through his mind, making him frown. He had just remembered something.

"Noah… I thought you would be happy?"

He sighed. "You had a letter from my father. He wants me to go home, doesn't he?"

Chapter Twenty

Aunt Margaret smiled reassuringly at him. "Oh, the letter. Yes, I nearly forgot. No – he isn't asking you to go home. Your father would like you to live with me for now. He has seen how unhappy you are. His wishes are for you to go to the boys' grammar school here, then go home during the holidays."

Noah held his breath.

"Well – do you think you could put up with your old aunt for a bit longer?"

Put up with Aunt Margaret? Live by a river? Go to a new school? No more liver? Rushing into her arms, he sobbed out his thanks.

She chuckled. "I take it that means yes. And, young man, no muddy feet on the carpets, or I will cast you out."

He brushed tears away and looked at her.

Her pretend stern face broke into a wide grin. "Your father does love you, Noah. That abrupt manner of his is just for show. He loved your mother, too. He tried to make her better, he really did – all the best treatments around, he consulted experts too but in the end he could do no more."

Noah looked at his feet. "I did blame him… but I think I know better now. I've changed."

"Yes. We have both changed."

"You, Aunt Margaret?"

"Yes, me too. I'm not sure now about getting married, at least not yet… but I've not said anything to Malcolm."

"Won't he be sad?"

"Yes, probably. It's having you here and finding out about Percy that's made me think. There are things I want to do before settling down. I would really like to use this school room for children who need help with their learning. I must have a chat with Percy when… if… he comes."

"Shall I go upstairs then, and wait until—"

"Certainly not. I am going right now. You will stay here in my Victorian schoolroom. If he comes, I will show him in and then leave you both to talk.

You can pass the time looking at the other photos in the scrapbook."

Aunt Margaret handed the scrapbook to Noah, and he thanked her, smiling at her as she left the room. He moved his chair nearer to the door and sat down, mouthing a silent prayer that Percy would come. He couldn't keep his eyes off the door. He didn't even want to look at the scrapbook for now; he must see Percy the very second he walked into the room – if he came at all. He must see Percy in Percy's own school room, where he had been happy, where he had become first a pupil, then a teacher, then a headmaster.

How unhappy Noah had been before he had met Percy. How different he felt about things now.

He sat still, not daydreaming, not thinking, not even seeing pictures; just allowing the sun to warm his soul.

After a while, he started to wonder if Percy wasn't coming after all.

That's when he heard a noise.

Was it footsteps, or had he imagined it? He listened. No – the steps were drawing nearer. The door handle was beginning to turn. The door was opening.

Who was it?

He caught his breath.

Walking into the room was an elderly man with a white scar that ran down his nose onto his top lip.

Holding out his hand, the man walked towards him.

As Noah stood up, he could hear the words of the river woman whispering, *"It is now complete."*

But for Noah, as he shook his old friend's hand, he knew the story was just beginning.

The End

Some Helpful History

Boarding schools

A boarding school is a school where children live and are educated whilst their parents live at home or abroad. Many but not all children go home during the holidays. All meals are provided. Children sleep in dormitories. Nursing care is given by a matron who is also in charge of all the domestic running of the school.

Steam trains in the 1930s

Noah travelled to his Aunt Margaret's house by steam train. Lots of small towns and even villages had their own railway station. Many of them were closed later on in the 1960s. This was because British Rail was losing money due to goods being transported by road instead of rail Also more people were buying cars to travel about in.

Noah would have been put on a train by an adult and allowed to travel on his own, knowing he was to be met by his aunt.

Victorian workhouses

Workhouses were large buildings for poor people who had no home or job or who were sick. Disabled people also lived there as well as children who had no parents. To earn their keep, people were given jobs.

Children had to work too, often long hours. The conditions were very harsh. There was no family life, as families who entered the workhouse were separated from each other. The inmates slept in dormitories. Beds were squashed together with not very much light. Men and women slept in separate dormitories as did children over the age of seven.

Each day was very much like the one before. All inmates wore uniforms and hardly ever had visitors. Food was more or less the same each day. Breakfast was porridge made with water or bread and cheese or vegetable broth. Dinner was stew made of beef or mutton with bread or suet pudding. Supper was often dry bread and cheese.

Children were given at least three hours of schooling a day, but it was very basic; simply reading, writing, arithmetic and the Christian religion.

Children would be starved of love. Many died in infancy, often from infections. Sometimes children who died in the workhouse were buried in mass graves.

So it is not surprising that Percy wanted to escape!

Children working in gangs

Children made to work in gangs often worked long days. This could be anything from 8 to 14 hours. When a gang was working some distance away the children may have had to leave at five in the morning and not return until eight at night.

The jobs they were given could be any sort of farm work including digging potatoes, clearing stones, and fruit picking. Eight was the usual age for children to be pressed into a gang, but seven was not unusual.

There is an account of a four-year-old girl who was taken by her father to the fields and put to work and a six-year-old boy who often walked more than six miles to work. Often he would come home so tired he could hardly stand up.

But help was to come for children made to work by gangmasters from a man named Lord Shaftesbury, who was born in London on 28 April 1801. He was a politician who cared for others and wanted to make life better for them. He persuaded the government to find out what was happening on some farms, and a report from the evidence of 500 witnesses was produced.

It reported that working in gangs damaged the health of young children. A bill was passed in 1867. Among other things it made it a crime for children under the age of eight to be employed on farms.

Sayings used in this book

- Afternoonified – smart or presentable.
- The morbs - depressed, down in the dumps

Victorian picnics

The Victorians loved picnics. There were always lots of different things to eat. Picnic baskets would be full to the brim. Meat and fish were the main foods including beef, ham, tongue, duck, fowl and lobster as well as meat pies and potatoes.

To follow there were lots of different puddings you could choose from such as fresh fruit, sweet steamed puddings, blancmange, jam puffs and cheesecakes. Drinks included homemade lemonade and ginger beer.

Sometimes people would play games after they had finished eating. No wonder Harold, Percy and Noah were sick!

The history of scrapbooks

In the 15th century, some people kept something called a 'commonplace book' which was filled with facts and ideas; things like herbal remedies, prayers, letters and wise sayings. By the 18th century these books would also contain paintings, poems and bits of writing. They were then called scrapbooks.

Keeping a scrapbook is a way of preserving memories. So it was the obvious choice for Percy to keep a record of the important events in his life. What an interesting way to tell Noah what had happened to him!

Adoption in the 19th century

Aunt Margaret was right. Even today, you don't need any legal paperwork in order to change your name! Anybody can call themselves anything they like, so long as there is no intention to commit fraud. Formal, legal adoption didn't start until the 1920s.

A pupil teacher

In Victorian times, sometimes older pupils were given the job of teaching the younger ones. They were given the title of 'pupil teacher' and were usually over the age of 13. After five years of being an apprentice they could call themselves a teacher.

So Percy must have worked very hard. I think he would have been a wonderful teacher. Maybe the children had lots of nature trips by the river.

Finally…

This is a work of fiction. In real life it can be dangerous to start a fire outdoors or play with fire. Also it can be dangerous to paddle in a river and drink water from a stream. Catching a trout is based on fact – but please don't try it without a grown-up!

About The Author

Anne Jordan lives in Leicestershire with her husband Paul. After becoming a Christian in her teens, Anne trained to be a primary teacher. After her children left home she became an adult education tutor, teaching people with learning difficulties and disabilities. She also taught creative writing to a class of adults who were recovering from mental health problems. Anne is now retired but has a heart for vulnerable children as well as a love of history.

She hopes you enjoyed reading this book. If you'd like to read the first in her *Lost At...* series, you can find *Lost At Home* on Amazon or buy it directly from her.

Printed in Dunstable, United Kingdom